I0586303

ASGARD'S DRAGON RIDER BOOKS

Valkyrie Academy Dragon Alliance

Series

Marked (Prequel)

Chosen

Vanished

Scorned

Inflicted

Empowered

Ambushed

Warned

Abducted

Besieged

Deceived

Thor's Dragon Rider Series

Safeguard

Pursuit

Entrapment

Hoodwinked

Relinquished

Shrouded

Assigned

Accosted

Destruction

EDITORIAL REVIEW

Thor's Dragon Rider
Book Seven

Assigned

"Kara and her fellow wingless Valkyries are tasked with a seemingly impossible mission, and they face obstacles and distractions at every turn. Can Kara outfox Loki and accomplish what Odin wants her to, or is she doomed to fail?" Susie D., Proofreader, Red Adept Editing

Assigned

Ebook first published in USA in April 2022 by Cosy Burrow
Books

Ebook first published in Great Britain in April 2022 by Cosy
Burrow Books

www.katrinacopebooks.com

Text Copyright © 2022 by Katrina Cope

Cover Design Copyright © art4artists.com.au

Published by Cosy Burrow Books

All rights reserved

ISBN : 978-0-6450874-8-2

❀ Created with Vellum

To the dream of riding a dragon.

BLURB

Assigned: Book 7 TDR

Blurb

An impossible task, a magic fiddler, and a trickster's interference.

Sent to Vanaheim to collect tears of grief, Kara is ordered by Odin to retrieve the goddess of youth and longevity. The goddess vanishes, muddying the additional task.

As if the mission weren't enough, Kara must overcome the spell of the alluring music or face a watery grave.

W*ait!*
Ready to haul myself onto Elan's back, I halt with one foot resting in the stirrup. "What is it?"

Panic shines in Tanda's red eyes, something I've never seen before in the red dragon, alerting me that something is wrong. I struggle to release my boot from the stirrup then stand on the ground to face the camel-humped dragon. The glow of concern in her eyes, which more often appear threatening, is disconcerting.

Tanda peers from side to side with wide eyes before twisting one hundred eighty degrees to check behind her back. When Britta's bonded dragon turns to face us again, her eyes are somehow wilder and more panicked. *Britta!* she exclaims as though that explains everything.

Quickly, I scan the darkness surrounding Yggdrasil's Helheim exit. "Where is she?" I frown, not yet understanding the red dragon's fever. Britta is a Valkyrie and more than able to defend herself. On top of that, we aren't in a threatening section of the underworlds.

The red dragon snorts out steam and spins in a full circle. *That's just it. I don't know. She was here a moment ago—now, she's gone. I can't see her anywhere in the dark.*

Tanda's panic is creeping under my skin as I attempt to search the nearby darkness again. Although Britta is welcome to travel away from the group, it isn't typical.

The leaves of the World Tree rustle in a soft breeze, and the coolness of the air adds to the tension, causing goose bumps to rise on the back of my neck. The mist brings dampness, making the air heavy. My capacity to see through the darkness lacks significantly compared to the dragons'.

A spray of mist lands on my face, and I wipe it away with a sleeve but find no assistance from the damp leather. The sensation adds irritation to my emotional mix. I slip a hand under Elan's scales to touch the soft skin underneath, ready to connect my vision with hers.

I can't see her either. Elan's mind speaking disrupts my hopeful thought, sending a flurry of concern to the depths of my stomach.

Zildryss rides on top of the golden dragon's head, clasping her horns with his front talons as he stretches to his full height and searches in every direction for the missing Valkyrie.

"Britta?" I shout and strain my ears, ready for an answer that doesn't come. "Britta?"

Eir, Hildr, and Thor join me in calling out as the dragons yell to the missing Valkyrie through their minds. Bile rises to my throat as I truly feel Tanda's panic. I heard no commotion or scuffle, none of the usual sounds of a Valkyrie being attacked or abducted. My friend has simply disappeared.

"She couldn't have just vanished into thin air," I say. "There must have been some sort of a struggle, or there must be a trace of where she went."

Naga will sniff her out. The blue dragon pushes through the other dragons, raising his nose and sniffing deeply. His nostrils flare and twitch until he suddenly spins, his tail flicking in our direction. We step back just in time as it slides across the ground in front of us and watch as he scurries, cutting between the dragons, and heads into the darkness.

A sword scrapes against its sheath as Hildr hustles to follow the smaller blue dragon. His head down and horns poised, ready to strike, Drogon follows protectively, his eyes alert, searching in all directions. Each group member folds into line and tracks Naga's progress, the blue dragon concentrating solely on Britta's scent. His path leads us from side to side, often halting to check that the smell remains fresh and contains Britta's essence before he scurries off in a slightly different direction.

Strangely, no signs of a struggle are evident. Something must've knocked the Valkyrie out and carried her away. No other explanation makes sense. Remaining alert, we progress farther yet not too far from the enormous trunk of Yggdrasil.

Elan's voice fills my head. *I can see drag marks.*

Zildryss squeaks, confirming he sees them also.

Then that would mean she was taken against her will, I say back through our bond then focus on the blue dragon. "Do you still have a scent, Naga?"

Yes. Naga still has the scent. He lifts his snout and sniffs to the left then to the right, his nostrils flaring and caving. *There is a strange smell with her, unlike anything Naga has smelled before.*

"Do you know if it's a creature or a person?" I ask.

The blue dragon's eyes hold a sadness as he shakes his head. *Naga doesn't know what is with her.*

Naga weaves and winds some more, and we follow like the tail end of a snake. While he is busy sniffing, the rest of the group studies the surrounding darkness for any sign of our friend. I think I see something behind us and peer over my shoulder to double-check. I run into something and brace myself just in time on Hildr's shoulders. Her body is tense, and her hand is wrapped firmly around her sword hilt, ready to attack.

"What is it?" I whisper.

"Drogon can hear something." She nods in the brown dragon's direction, and I follow her indication, spotting the multihorned dragon snorting out hot air, his talons scraping across the ground.

"What is it, Drogon?" I whisper.

I don't know. I don't know what I'm hearing. The horns on the brown dragon's forehead bunch together as he frowns. He glances at Elan. *Can you tell what it is?*

Elan screws up her face, and some of her golden scales cluster in a lump. *It sounds like chanting.* Her head tilts to one side. *Almost tribal.* She straightens her back. *That's concerning. I didn't know there were tribes down here.*

"As far as I know, there aren't any tribes down here." Thor's voice grows louder as he approaches from behind.

Eir steps into line with us. "Then what else could it be?"

Thor's broad shoulders lift into a shrug. "There's only one way to find out."

The chanting crescendos as we progress, my heart aching with worry for our friend. Darkness and fog shroud the surroundings as Naga leads us around a bend. The blue dragon pauses midstride, and Drogon accidentally rams him from behind and pushes him forward, causing the blue dragon to dig in his talons.

Drogon cringes and pulls back. *Sorry, little guy.*

Naga appears undeterred and plants his concerned blue eyes on the larger brown dragon. *There's something around the corner, and the scent here is much stronger than before.*

Stealthily, the three Valkyries and Thor tiptoe and peer around Naga. With each step, the chanting grows louder, and a dull light grows. Still not seeing enough, I move around the dragon and skim the edge of the trunk of the enormous World Tree and halt when I glimpse the source of the light. The chanting drums in my ears.

Away from the trunk, a sizeable stone-enforced well is illuminated by the golden glow of a campfire. A large root of Yggdrasil arches over the stone edges and plunges into the center of the water. Several other roots line the ground in scattered patterns.

Three haggard women have covered their severely wrinkled skin in dark cloaks. They dance and chant, circling around the well, and a hideous chuckle cuts short one of the chants. The hairs on my arms rise. They sound like witches.

The woman that chuckled tosses her head back for a second time as she cackles again. "I like this one. I like this one a lot." Her voice is raspy yet undisturbed as she circles the well and continues her tribal dancing. "This one has great pain in her past." She rubs her hands together. "Yes, great pain."

My searching eyes land on Britta. A strap covers the Valkyrie's mouth, and her eyes are open, her body tied against the well wall. Every now and then, these haggard women reach into the well and splash water over our friend, and Britta's face crinkles with displeasure.

Intrigue washing her face, the woman following the cackling woman asks, "What is it about this one, Wyrd? Why do you like this one so much? What pain is in her past?"

The third woman watches Wyrd keenly, and when she doesn't answer immediately, she says, "Tell us, sister. Tell us!" She rubs her hands together in anticipation, the movement highlighting her spindly shoulders through the large cloak. "Tell us what is in her past."

Great! Britta's been kidnapped by three nutcases.

Nodding, I agree with Elan's point. Something is odd about these three. I sense Elan's presence towering over me, but she is nowhere to be seen when I turn. She must have gone invisible.

Thor whispers, "These are the Norns. They protect the Yggdrasil and keep it alive. They are vital to the survival of the connecting realms."

"Oh. I've read about them," Eir whispers. "Don't they also tell people's fate?"

Thor nods. "That is the belief. Many swear by their prophecies."

"You don't sound too convinced," Hildr remarks.

Thor wiggles his head from one side to the other. "I am, but I'm not. I can't speak from experience."

The first Norn chuckles, lifts her worn skirt, and kicks her legs, exposing their malnourished thinness. Still, her movements are swift as she dances. "This one has suffered much pain, much prejudice. You see, you see. She lacks the wings of a Valkyrie." She grasps Britta's shoulders as though to pull her forward to expose her wingless back.

Britta yanks back and presses against the rocks of the well, which only causes the strange woman to cackle again.

"Her sorrow is deep and full of grief," the woman says. "This one is fueled by the pains of the past. Yes."

My jaw drops. It's not news to us that Britta has felt pain about this. All the wingless Valkyries have pain from the past, but these women seem to be rejoicing over that, which doesn't sit right with me. Not only that, they've also kidnapped our friend. I don't know how they managed to capture Britta, an adept fighter who could easily take down many beings, especially those as frail and weak as these three, yet something is off about their appearances. Having come from Helheim, I've learned not to judge a being's strength by size and looks. I have seen some powerful skeletons.

One of the sisters grabs a bucket of water out of the well and pours it over one of the roots surrounding the well. "There you go, Yggdrasil. Drink it up." She then returns the bucket to the side of the well and flicks drops of the well water over Britta's head, earning a scowl from the Valkyrie. That only seems to encourage the Norn.

"What do we do?" Eir whispers from next to me, her peaceful face pale in the dull light.

We charge! Drogon lowers his enormous head, aiming his abundant horns, and charges into their ritual.

Chapter Two

"**D**rogon!" I hiss.

Hildr barges past, following her dragon.

"Hildr!"

She also ignores my call.

Elan's hot breath warms my back as I charge after the brown dragon and his rider, our element of surprise gone.

Does that dragon ever think first? Elan groans in frustration. Her thundering footsteps follow close behind that she almost towers over me, and this comforts me.

Zildryss squeaks his disapproval, still hanging onto Elan's horns, his lilac tail swinging wildly.

Hildr and Drogon don't know what they're dealing with, but as usual, the hotheads have already acted. We're all keen to rescue Britta, yet I'm sure we could have devised a better way to go about it.

Drogon's thundering footsteps dampen the

women's chanting. Their dancing abruptly halts when the brown dragon swings his tail and thumps it on the ground like a morning star, lodging the spikes deep into the dirt. He maneuvers the rest of his body to block any threat to Britta and growls, tiny wisps of flame sneaking through his teeth. Tanda charges to Drogon's tail side, blocking the women from our friend.

My heart warms. Each of these bonded dragons will protect their bonded and their friends. Relief washes over Britta's face as she gazes at the defending dragons and the shield they've built around her.

Hildr advances to the nearest woman, and her target turns, exposing her full waifish form to us. She is aged and extremely frail, as though she hasn't eaten well for quite some time. She appears as though she would break easily.

Hildr holds her sword up to the woman's neck, her other hand raised, and fingers stroking a ball of magic, poised and ready to fire. "What do you want from my friend?"

The woman chuckles, producing a look of confusion on Hildr's face. "It's not me who wants her. It's Wyrd, my sister." The aged woman points a gnarled finger over the well. "It is her. She wants her."

With her attention drawn to the woman across the

well, Hildr's captive pushes the sword away from her skin, her fingers touching the flat side of the blade. Distracted, Hildr is unaware that her sword is moving. Drogon flicks his tail, landing it at the woman's feet, and she drops her hands.

Suddenly, Wyrd's body goes rigid, and her back thumps against the well. Eir stomps toward the woman, her boots pounding menacingly, one hand poised and ready to throw another blast of magic at the secured woman. The ancient woman's body is pinned, only her eyes and face moving.

"Who do you think you are?" Resolve thickens the peaceful Valkyrie's voice.

The secured woman chuckles loudly, bearing an air of nonchalance like her sister. "We are the Norns. Have you not heard of us?" When Eir maintains her threatening position, the woman continues, "We are the three Norn sisters, the guardians of the Well of Urd, which feeds the Yggdrasil." With her limbs sill frozen in place, she must make an effort to gaze over her shoulder at the well. "That well behind me is the one we have to guard. If it weren't for us, the Yggdrasil would die, and your realms would cease to exist."

"Yes, I have heard of you." The peaceful Valkyrie's face twitches in what looks like annoyance, making me wonder where my gentle friend has disappeared to. She has, however, become more aggressive when her friends are in danger. "If you are protectors, then why did you take our friend?"

"Oh, my dear. We only guard the Well of Urd and Yggdrasil, not everything else. Besides, your friend's pain captured my attention. I could sense it from here. Yes. Yes. Pain." Her eyebrow twitches, and she tilts her head to one side, observing Eir. "And I can sense you have felt it too, deep pain." Wyrd's eyes flick to Hildr then me. "Yes. Yes. You have. All of you have a deep, deep pain."

The sister in front of Hildr chuckles, inciting the Valkyrie to reinforce her attacking position. The blade focused on her neck only makes the Norn chuckle more loudly. "Yes. That is Wyrd's specialty. She loves to find the pain of the past. As for you"— the woman's dark eyes bear down on Hildr—"you have pain in your immediate future." The Norn's eyes seem to dance with pleasure while she observes Hildr's discomfort.

The third Norn on the other side of the well claps her hands. "Yes. Tell her, Verdandi. Tell her." She shuffles eagerly from side to side. "Tell her. We want to hear." Her smile exposes her missing top teeth. "We want to hear what this one is going to face in the near future. What is she going to face, to face?"

Hildr's captive tucks her chin, and the hood from

her cloak casts a deep shadow over her eyes. Her pleasure at Hildr's demise remains clear in her wide grin, which exposes crooked brown teeth. "How fitting you should choose me," she says.

"I didn't choose you," Hildr growls. "You were the closest one."

"That was fate, was fate," Verdandi says. "Fate directed you to me, to me, so that I may expose your near future. Yes, yes. Your near future."

The third sister, at the back of the well, shuffles from side to side, clapping her hands again with a delighted cackle. "Tell her, Verdandi. Tell her, tell her."

Drogon growls, and Hildr's obvious annoyance only encourages the woman.

"Tell her, Verdandi. Predict her near future. Tell her. Tell her. I want to hear what's so bad in her future. Wyrd has found something drastic in our captive's past. We want to hear that one's near future." She points at Hildr.

Wyrd joins her sister in the chorus. "We want to hear about the bad in her near future."

I cringe. Their repetitiveness is getting on my nerves along with the fact that they seem pleased to hold something drastic over Hildr's future.

"Fine." Hildr lowers her sword. "Anything to shut you lot up. Whatever she tells me is probably rubbish anyway. I don't believe in this mumbo jumbo. We know Britta has had a troubled past. It's common knowledge that she has been troubled by her lack of wings. What wingless Valkyrie hasn't?" She lowers the hand that was loaded with magic, places it on her hip, and twirls her sword with practiced precision. "Go on. Tell me."

"It's my pleasure." Verdandi smiles broadly, leaving me surprised that the phrase wasn't repeated. "Your mission shall fail, shall fail."

"Right!" Hildr lets out a loud, frustrated sigh. "What mission? I go on lots of missions."

Still pressed against the side of the well by Eir's magic, Wyrd laughs. "She doesn't get it, sister. She doesn't get what you said. We can't have that, now, can we? Tell her again. Tell her. The prophecy of the near future. Tell her, tell her."

"Your mission in the near future will fail, will fail," the Norn says again.

Hildr shakes her head and drops her sword back into its sheath. "These lot are just a bunch of loonies. I believe they're harmless, other than abducting Britta. Untie Britta, and let's get going."

His red eyebrows descending like thunderclouds, Thor slams his hammer onto the ground, his eyes constricting with anger at the Norns. He trudges to the center of the commotion with earth-rumbling footsteps. "Why did you Norns steal Britta?"

"We wanted to help free her from her pain, her pain." Wyrd holds up her freed hands.

"It's not okay to just take her like that." Thor thrust a muscled arm in Hildr's direction. "I suppose you're going to say that you are trying to take away Hildr's pain too."

"Not in this case, this case. No. That one's pain is different. We are just exposing its coming. We are sealing its fate." Verdandi reaches into the well and splashes water over Hildr's face.

Hildr screws up her nose and pulls back. "Hey! What was that for?"

Verdandi grins. "It's confirming the prophecy, prophecy."

Hildr wipes her face with a leather sleeve. "Whatever. I guess I'll just have to wait and see if yours comes true. But I doubt it."

A worried look passes over Thor's face. "I just hope they aren't talking about your next mission, Hildr." His voice is deep and gravelly, barely audible.

"I'm not going to lie. Making everyone in the Yggdrasil realms shed a sincere tear for Balder isn't going to be easy." A deep sadness passes over Hildr's face before she forces it away. She aggressively thumps a fist against her other palm and smirks slyly.

"But I'll find a way. Come on. Let's go." Hildr helps Britta off the ground before we all turn to leave.

"Wait!"

I turn to see the third sister pull her hand out of the well and flick water onto my face also before I realize what is happening.

- Chapter Three -

I stumble back a few paces, and the ancient woman follows me with an extended hand.

A maleficent grin covers the woman's wrinkled face. "Ah, yes. Yes!"

Verdandi eagerly throws back her hood, exposing her long gray tatty hair. "Tell her, Skuld. Tell her what it is. I want to hear. I want to hear."

Displeased to be the focus of their attention, I push my mouth to one side. Also, the Norns' constant repetitiveness is getting on my nerves even more.

"Yes," Skuld says.

Her pursuit of me is eerie. She doesn't appear to want to physically harm me. The sisters only seem to wish to cause us grief. Longing for them to finish their theatrics, I push aside the discomfort they radiate and stand firm.

Skuld flashes her decaying teeth. "Ah yes. That's

better." She hovers around me as though assessing me from all directions. "Ooh." Her shoulders rise with excitement. "Your future holds great disappointment. Agreed, great disappointment."

My mouth twitches. "Oh yeah? And what would that be?"

She doesn't seem put off by my skepticism. Her eyes closed, Skuld waves one clawed hand in the direction of my head, rocking back and forth as though trying to draw information out via magic. "You have such great missions, such great missions. And responsibility—yes, yes, lots of responsibility." After opening her eyes, she glances at Thor before focusing back on me. "There is great value in your future. What you attempt to achieve is very great. There will be many pitfalls, oh yes, many pitfalls."

I shrug. "All right. That sounds like my normal life. What exactly are you referring to?"

"You will lose something that the gods hold in high respect." Her eyebrows quirk. "Yes, yes, you will lose what is precious to them. You will lose what they hold dear." She claps her hands. "Ha-ha. Oh, this is delightful! So delightful!"

Her relishing in my failure is disconcerting, but as this seems normal for any of their subjects, I push my shoulders back. "There isn't anything new in your so-called prophecy. I am constantly disappointing

Odin. As long as my friends are safe and I don't lose anybody important to me or them, then that's okay." I turn to leave.

"Ah, but you will. You will. You will lose someone important to you. You will lose someone you're trying to protect. Great sadness is coming your way. Great sadness."

My heart sinks as my thoughts wander. Since I can lose anyone I care about, I wonder why I'm fighting so hard to protect my friends and realm if I'm going to disappoint, fail, and lose someone precious.

"Wait a second." Thor interrupts my thoughts. "You usually only have one prophecy. Which one is it? From what you have said, basically, her whole future is all doom and gloom." He places a firm hand on my shoulder. "I know this Valkyrie well, and this isn't how she works. Not everything is a win, but overall, she succeeds. I find it extremely difficult to believe that her whole future is doomed. So which one is the correct one?"

Skuld casts Thor a sideways glance from under an arched stringy eyebrow. "I have heard about you and what you have achieved." She leans in close, pinches my cheek, and tugs at it. At this distance, her wrinkled face appears to be aged leather. "But what I say is true.

All is true. Yes, all is true. It is usually one prophecy that we predict." She scratches behind an ear, and a clump of unwashed gray hair catches in her fingers and falls over her face. "But as you said, this one is special, and many failures and disappointments are coming her way. Ha-ha. Many failures and disappointments."

I pull back and trip over Thor's large boot. His strong hand grasps my upper arm before I fall.

"All right!" Authority laces Thor's voice. "That's enough. You three sisters have had your fun with this group. We're leaving."

"But wait!" the sisters call at once.

Thor expels an annoyed sigh. "What is it?"

The Norn sisters scurry to the well and flick water over the prophesied people. I flinch back, knowing this is how they seal the outcome, but I'm too slow. Nervous, I wipe the water away with my leather sleeve, hoping that limiting its time on my skin will tamper with the "doomed" outcome.

"The Yggdrasil thanks you for your service," the Norns say in unison, and cold despair settles in my stomach.

"Okay. I've had enough of crazy." Hildr turns to leave as Drogon soaks the Norns with steam before marching behind her.

Thor grabs Sleipnir's reins, tugging him to follow

Hildr and Drogon. "I agree. I'm pretty sure it's time to go."

We leave the area with a sense of doom clouding over our heads. With all my strength, I hold onto the hope that what they've said won't come true. Britta's reading was indeed accurate, but it's the past, not a secret from the realms of the Yggdrasil. Its truth doesn't mean the rest of it will come true. I don't want Hildr to fail on any mission, nor do I want to lose any friends or disappoint any other gods. I study Thor from behind, hoping he won't lose faith in me and be disappointed. I look forward to the day that this menace is over, and the peril of Ragnarok is obviated. Each time we move forward to remove the threat, we are sent on side missions, distracting us.

As though sensing my worry, Elan nudges me from behind. *We will get through whatever happens. Do not worry yourself. It will only make it harder for you to focus on what needs to be done.*

I fall back into line with her, placing a hand on her nose. *Thanks for always being there for me, Elan. My life would be nothing without you.*

She leans her head into me. *I feel the same about you. You have turned me into a better potential leader and opened my eyes to things I would never see in the dragon wastelands.*

Zildryss flies down from the crown of Elan's head

and loops around my neck, pressing his warm under-belly against my skin. I rest my head briefly on his back.

Slowly, we travel in silence back to our exit from Helheim into the World Tree, ready to separate into different realms and undertake our mission of retrieving tears for Balder.

The clopping of Sleipnir's hooves halts as Thor pauses at the entrance of Yggdrasil. "I wish everyone the best of luck. Wipe away what those weird women have said and pursue your mission to the best of your ability. I know you'll give it your all, and I have faith in all of you." His gaze falls on me. "We have defeated obstacles that seemed impossible in the past, and we will keep doing this."

Sleipnir carries the god of thunder into the Yggdrasil, and they disappear to the realms of Niflheim, Muspelheim, and Helheim. His task of covering the three realms shouldn't take him too long, for hardly any beings are alive in these realms.

Hildr mounts Drogon, wrapping the reins around one hand. "I'll see you guys on the other side." Drogon leaps into Yggdrasil's trunk and flies up to Midgard.

Eir moves to the edge of the tree trunk.

I nudge Eir and smirk. "You'd better be going to

visit your love interest while you're on Alfheim. It's about time you got to see him again."

Eir tucks her chin, and even in the darkness, I can see a flash of color fill her cheeks. "I certainly hope so. But it won't be a time of relaxation and pleasure. We must try to get Balder back where he belongs."

She gives me a hug. I'm not usually the hugging type, but separating to go to different realms and dangers bears heavily on us.

Naga nudges me with his muzzle. *Naga will make sure Eir spends lots of time with him. She needs to settle with a mate. Naga knows she isn't getting any younger. It would make Naga very happy to see little Eirs.*

The color in Eir's cheeks grows. "Naga!"

Naga flashes his large array of teeth. *Take care, Kara, Elan, Britta, and Tanda, okay? Naga and Eir will miss you.*

I rub his nose. "And we will miss you, Naga and Eir."

Zildryss scurries around Naga's head and drags his body down the blue dragon's nose before flying to my shoulders.

Naga will miss Zildryss too.

Zildryss makes a couple of strange squeaks and tilts his head to one side while looking at the blue dragon as though saying the same.

Eir climbs onto Naga's back, and they disappear into the hole.

I expel a sigh. Even though they've just left, I already miss my friends. "Okay, Britta. Are you ready?"

"As ready as I can be." She climbs onto Tanda.

I hoist myself onto Elan's saddle, and we push through the hole and into the darkness of Yggdrasil's trunk. Instantly, the dragons take us upward, heading toward the top layers of the World Tree.

Vanaheim. Here we come, Elan calls.

- Chapter Four -

We burst through a hole, exiting the World Tree's trunk, welcomed by fresh air filled with the scent of leaves and water.

Elan launches into the sky, narrowly missing a low-hanging branch. *If I've calculated properly, this should be Vanaheim.* She circles and touches down with Tanda landing next to her.

Dragon scales! Tanda's bright-red eyes were wide, taking in the scenery. *Now I understand why we don't see too many Vanir gods on Asgard. This place is amazing. It's like everything has a glow. Everything seems so pristine and pretty. Stunning!*

Britta huffs. "That and the fact that the Asir and Vanir gods often fight."

Really? Tanda asks then cocks her head to one side. *Actually, that doesn't surprise me. Many of the gods are quite conceited and have difficulty empathizing with other creatures. I've learned from experience and would still be experiencing it, if not for Elan and Kara.* Her red eyes soften as she looks at us.

Britta rubs the skin under her scales. "You were treated poorly when you were captured under Odin's authority. All the captured dragons were. I'm also grateful that things have changed, and you can be my bonded dragon."

Tanda stretches her long neck over her shoulder and nuzzles Britta's leg. *I'd never have it any other way.*

Their friendship warms my heart. Through our bond, I send my overwhelming love to Elan while running a hand over her rough golden scales shining brightly in the Vanaheim light. I would never have dreamed that my life could change so much, largely because this wonderful, wise, and witty dragon decided to watch over me. Elan's love for me returns through the bond and seeps deep into my body, comforting my tired muscles.

I lift my gaze and study the realm of Vanaheim, which is precisely as Tanda said. Mountains display several cascading waterfalls under pure-blue sky broken only by fluffy white clouds sparkling under the sun. Not only the clouds sparkle. Everything in this realm seems to glisten, as though the beauty inside needs to shine out. Deep valleys line tall mountains, and a forest rests far to our left. Birds sing their choruses loudly from the branches of Yggdrasil, answering calls in the distant forest. The walls of a small city shine on the right, seemingly built of gold.

Britta's gaze narrows on the city. "It almost seems a bit too much."

"It is a place for the Vanir gods. They seem a little bit vainer than Asgard's gods. Looking at the way the realm presents itself, I'm not surprised that the Vanir gods focus on their looks." I grasp Elan's reins more tightly. "I need to stretch my legs."

In one motion, I sling a leg over Elan's back and drop to the ground before unhooking my other foot from the stirrup. My arrows rattle in their quiver strapped on my back, and I feel my sword's sheath tucked flush against my back as I move away from the tree trunk. The crackling sounds of the grass under my boots are drowned out by a nasal voice behind me.

"Wait!"

Cringing, I slowly turn around. I know that if I don't stop, the squirrel will follow me anyway.

Poised on the branch above me, his fur glimmering in the sunshine, is Ratatoskr. Even the red in his coat seems to glow more brightly in this realm.

Placing my hands on my hips, I call up to the rodent, "What is it now, Ratatoskr?"

His beady black eyes narrow as he peers down at

me. "What? No friendly greeting for the one and only messenger?"

I huff. "I'll give you a friendly greeting when you deserve it."

Britta moves to my side, glaring up at the rodent. "Respect and friendliness are not rights."

Ratatoskr waves a dismissive paw at us. "Yeah, yeah. The same old story."

I grunt. "What is it, Ratatoskr? We have a mission to fulfill, leaving us with a lot to do. We don't have time for your games."

Ratatoskr huffs. "What's the rush?"

"We have to get a lot of people to cry for Balder and his passing," Britta says. "It's the only way that Hel will release him from Helheim. Someone like him needs to be given a chance for an honorable death."

I grab a vial from my pack. "Which reminds me. We need you to shed a tear for Balder and his early passing." I hold the empty vial out. "Just drop your tear in here. If you do it now, it will save us a trip to find you later."

"Oh. Boo-hoo," Ratatoskr says without a scrap of sympathy. He arches his back and caves his chest, feigning a forlorn look. "I'm crying so hard."

Britta crosses her arms. "No. We need you to cry a

genuine tear for Balder, not make up some sarcastic, unheartfelt cry."

"Pfft! Well, then. You will have continue without a tear from me," the red squirrel says, seeming undeterred.

Displeasure radiates from my every pore. "Why's that?"

"Haven't you heard? Squirrels can't cry." Ratatoskr leans in closer and directs his words with a paw, half cupping his mouth in our direction. "And guess what? In case you didn't know, I'm a squirrel."

More like a rat, Tanda says.

Elan giggles softly through mind speak, and my heart is right there with her.

Ratatoskr wobbles his head. "Ha-ha. Very funny. But I'm sure you're not expected to get a tear from a being that can't cry." He flails his arms out to his sides. "I can't cry. Plain and simple. How else can I explain it?"

I scowl. "Then why are you here?"

As always, Ratatoskr ignores my annoyance and gazes down his pointy nose at me. "Odin has sent me."

"And what insult is Odin sending me this time?" I ask.

"Oh, the usual." He dusts his claws on his white-furred chest.

The urge to strangle the little creature grows stronger, and sucking in a deep, calming breath takes a great effort. "Can you be more specific?"

The rodent chuckles. "Okay. You asked for it." He straightens his back and wriggles his shoulders. "Odin says you're the dumbest being ever. He sends you on a simple mission to retrieve his son, yet you still have failed."

"Hang on a minute," Britta interrupts. "We were all sent on the mission, including Thor. It's not just Kara's responsibility."

Ratatoskr shrugs. "I'm just passing on the message, and this is the message Odin wants to send to Kara." He slaps a palm to his forehead. "I mean, he was right there within your grasp. You could have just grabbed him, put him on your dragon, and dragged him home." He waggles a claw at me. "Odin is not impressed."

"We couldn't just grab and take him home," I protested. "Hel had to release him."

Ratatoskr places his paws on his hips. "Well, clearly, you weren't good enough to convince Hel to let him go."

"What do you think we're doing here?" Britta asks, her voice high-pitched. "We struck a bargain with Hel, and we are attempting to execute it."

Ratatoskr leans against the tree trunk and crosses his legs. "You'd better hurry, then."

I groan. "We're trying. You're holding us up." I back away. "I'm going!"

"Wait!" Ratatoskr calls. "I haven't given you the message yet."

Calling over my shoulder, I say, "Oh, I thought the insult was the message. It usually is."

The squirrel blurts out, "Odin has demanded that you find someone."

Scowling, I turn to face him. "I thought Odin wasn't happy with my service. Why would he send me on extra missions if he thinks I don't succeed at anything?"

The squirrel shrugs. "I guess he's giving you another chance. Who knows why? He wants you to bring Idun back to Asgard when you return."

Frowning, I ask, "And who is Idun? I've never even heard of them. Are they a she or a he?" I fling my arms out in frustration.

"Perhaps you should do some research." Ratatoskr turns and disappears back into Yggdrasil's hole.

Annoyed, I spin around and walk toward the rest of Vanaheim and the buildings in the distance. A flash of lilac flies around my head and lands on my shoulders. Zildryss flicks out a tongue at an insect.

The strike narrowly misses as the insect swerves to one side. The tiny lilac dragon has another go, and again the insect manages to dodge. Its buzzing increases, growing louder as though the insect is protesting the little dragon's attacks.

Zildryss tilts his head to the side and licks one eye then the other, watching the insect as it flies to the ground and morphs.

My footsteps falter. I'm stunned at what lies before me.

Chapter Five

"**L**oki!" The name escapes my lips before I can stop it.

He bows slightly, a wry smile dancing on his face. "Well, of course."

It feels like he's mocking me, playing with my mind, and causing me to remember all the times he's deceived me. My eyes narrow. "Have you been hanging around and spying on us in different forms?"

His sardonic smile broadens.

"Never mind," I say when he doesn't confirm or deny. "How did you escape from your cell?"

He arches an eyebrow. "I have my ways. You should know me better than that by now."

Britta shoulders in front of me as though trying to protect me from any further emotional harm. "What are you doing here? Aren't you the one who put Balder in Helheim in the first place?"

Loki shrugs, looking sheepish, and my blood turns cold.

Britta reaches forward to clasp his hands. "Have you come to turn yourself in?"

Loki avoids her grasp with a quick flick and steps back with his arms raised. Falling to his shoulders, his dark hair matches his tight leather cloak cinched at his shoulders and waist and flowing to his calves. "Now, hang on. Not so fast. I've come to give you a hand."

I grit my teeth. "We don't want your help."

Loki moves his hands in a calming motion. "I overheard what little Ratatoskr said, and despite what you think, it sounds like you need my help."

Britta crosses her arms and leans on one leg. "Really? And how do you think you can help us?"

Loki smiles, showing off his perfectly aligned teeth, expressing that charm I no longer find endearing. "I can help you find Idun. I know what she looks like."

My interest piques. "So it's a she?"

Amusement dances in his eyes. "Why, yes."

Feeling like I'm being mocked, I cross my arms over my chest.

"Why is she so important to Odin?" Britta asks.

Loki clasps his hands behind his back and paces, reminding me of forms he has taken in the past when adopting the role of a teacher. "You see, Idun is the provider of immortality and youth."

Britta tugs testily on her long ponytail, her impatience a reflection of my own. "What do you mean?"

The mischievous god runs a hand through his hair. "Idun provides a special fruit to the gods, similar to an apple, that delivers immortality and youth." He smirks. "You've seen Odin. You can't deny that he needs a little of that youth."

When we only respond with frowns, he shrugs. "Perhaps his wife Frigg has become quite ugly in her grief."

My mouth drops open. "Hey! That's not nice!"

The mischievous god clasps his hands and rocks on his toes. "I was just saying the obvious. In my opinion, Idun is highly overrated. From what I hear, she doesn't have the best morals and has lain with her brother's murderer."

Dragon scales! That's disgusting! We don't need to know that! Elan towers over the god, breathing steam over him and causing sweat to rise on his forehead.

A look of displeasure spreads over his pointy features, and he pulls a white handkerchief out of an inside cloak pocket to wipe away the sweat. "There is no need for that. After all, you need me." He plasters on his charming smile again.

Elan snorts more steam on him then sits on her

backside, straightening her back. *I'm just giving you the respect you deserve.*

Never mind that. Can I eat him and rid us of his presence forever? Tanda licks her big lips.

Loki's thin face turns expressionless. He swallows, his eyes narrowing before he speaks through clenched teeth. "Right! I see how it is. I'd prefer it if you didn't eat me. Although I'd like to see you try. I do have a trick or two that will put you off."

Tanda snorts. *Like what?*

A wry smile crosses the god's face. "Like turning into a cabbage. I'm sure you wouldn't enjoy the taste of that."

Tanda screws up her nose. *You can do that?*

"Try to eat me, and you'll find out." When she shakes her head, he dusts his hands together. "That's settled, then. If you insist on mistreating me, I could leave you to find Idun on your own. In any case, you need me if you don't know who Idun is."

The thought of needing Loki's help doesn't sit right with me. Even so, I have to admit I don't have a clue where to start. I gaze up at the fluffy white clouds creating patterns in the brilliant blue sky, pondering what to do. The light of Vanaheim makes them appear sparkly and golden. Perhaps I can force him to assist in order to make up for some of his past wrongdoings. I could certainly use some help to impress Odin. Clearly, I'm still in the doghouse from accidentally releasing Loki from his enchanted bindings in that cave, and I need to make up for it.

"Shall we proceed?" Loki pulls me from my contemplation. "I must admit I'm not a fan of Vanaheim, but I will help."

I study him, unable to discern his motives, because thinking of others without an ulterior motive is not in his nature. "Why would you help?"

"Ah, Kara." He reaches for my shoulder, making me swerve away. Ignoring my rejection, he continues, "I have always placed you in high regard. Unlike the other Valkyries I've known, you have created such a loyal following. You've even managed to convince the dragons and Valkyries to unite, unlike any other beings I know. I could never have connected with my dragons like you've connected with yours."

Elan grumbles. *No surprise there. You were stealing them from their families and only using them for war.*

Loki talks through his teeth. "Oh, Elan. Even though you're the next in line to lead the dragons of the wastelands, you have so much to learn. There are several concealed things to consider."

Elan nods. *That is true, and it is why I'm still my mother's understudy. I will never forgive you for stealing the dragons' eggs from the wasteland. And I doubt any other dragons will, either.*

Tanda snarls in agreement.

Elan indicates the red dragon with her head. *See?*

"I understand," Loki says. "But just remember there's always more to me than what you want to see."

What? You're saying you're more than a treacherous beast? Pfft! Elan retracts her head in shock.

"I admit I do have several layers, and sometimes the competitive side can appear that way." He turns toward Vanaheim, gazing over the buildings in the distance. "Shall we proceed?"

Without waiting for an answer, he weaves his way down the hill, leading us deep within the valley, which is rolling with ground cover, a blanket of green and bright flowers of different colors. The plants roll up the sides of the breathtaking mountains, which spill out glorious cascades of waterfalls. The scenery rivals the sparkling beauty of nature in Alfheim, and here, the walls of their city glisten like gold in the sun.

"How come we aren't taught about the beauty of this place on Asgard?" I ask. "It should be something we learn at the academy."

"Didn't they teach you at the academy that the Vanir and the Asir are often enemies?" Studying our blank faces, Loki continues, "Obviously not. It's because of this that they don't tell you. The Asir gods would hate to admit that the Vanir have a better realm."

"Are you trying to tell us we're entering enemy territory?" Britta's hand wavers over her sword hilt, reminding me of Hildr, which makes me instantly miss the quick-to-anger Valkyrie.

Loki's breath is ragged as he ascends the hill and talks over his shoulder. "The Asir and the Vanir are currently in a peace agreement. But don't expect either to praise the other without having to."

Having dealt with a few gods, I'm not surprised by what he says. The majority of the gods are conceited and self-important. Things would likely only be worse while Odin was in charge.

As I climb the steep mountainside, my legs burn, and my ears want to mute the god of mischief. He won't stop talking and trying to act like we're still friends.

Loki slows his ascent and turns to me. "So, how is your magic training going?"

I scowl. "What? Are you trying to see how much I know in case you have to combat me sometime soon?"

He throws back his head and chuckles. "I wasn't worried about that. I was merely seeing if I could teach you anything while we look for Idun."

Narrowing my eyes, I huff. "Why don't you just

shut that mouth of yours and mind your own business?"

His grin spreads wider, which irks me. "That can be arranged. Well, not the minding my own business, but I can teach you how to shut someone up."

Britta holds up a large stick as though ready to swing it. "By clobbering them over the head?"

Quickly, Loki sidesteps out of reach. "Actually, by magic. I can teach you too."

The Valkyrie throws the stick aside. "If I can use it on you, sure."

The god pauses. "You can try."

"Why do you even want to teach us anything, anyway?" I grumble.

He shrugs. "Simple. I'm the reason why you received your magic in the first place. I feel the responsibility to refine and teach you more."

I cross my arms. Other than on Alfheim, I haven't had anyone else to teach me magic, and I know I have more to learn. "Fine! Yo—" I clasp my throat as my words stop coming, though my mouth moves. I feel no pain, only shock that I'm unable to speak.

Britta notices my distress. "What did you do to her?"

Loki grins. "Why, I stopped her from talking." He flicks his fingers discreetly, and my voice clears.

I stop grasping at my throat. "Teach us, then."

"Easy. All you do is concentrate on the person's voice box and imagine your magic wrapping around it, stopping the sound from exiting." He holds up a hand and elegantly twists his fingers. "Then you just twist your fingers like so, controlling the magic with th—"

Before he can finish his sentence, I execute the move on him. He catches sight of my twisting fingers and smiles then twists his own fingers in the opposite direction.

"Very good!" he says.

"Wha—"

He cuts off my words again, making me scowl. "Relax. I'm able to undo the spell on myself. You learned quickly. I'm impressed."

I twist my fingers, undoing his spell on my voice box. "Such a shame we can't use it to shut you up permanently."

Loki chuckles. "In your dreams. Now, it's time for you to try, Britta."

Britta doesn't take very long either. The spell is a simple one to execute. We practice many times as we continue climbing the hill and only stop when Loki leads us through the golden gates of the city.

- Chapter Six -

At each step we take into the city after Loki, I wonder when he will betray us next. My skin tingles with anticipation, as I'm confident that treachery will come soon or that he will leave us stranded in an awkward position. I don't understand whatever motivation causes him to constantly change his mind about his alliances. Just thinking about it sends my head into a spiral of confusion.

The glistening walls of the city streets close in around us, allowing enough room for a carriage to pass through. Seeing the walls up close, I realize they're made from pale marble, and only the unique rays of the sun shining in Vanaheim give them the appearance of gold. Even the streets, carved from the same stone, shine up at us, seeming to light the way.

Loki's path leads us toward a courtyard with a large flowing fountain in the center. A statue of a beautiful goddess stands in it, large pots tilted from her shoulder and waist, pouring water back into the source. Her well-proportioned body is covered with folds of stone fabric tapered at the waist and pinned to one shoulder. The crystal-clear water shimmers brightly around the goddess in the sunlight.

Several women pass by, wearing beautiful flowing dresses similar to the statue goddess's. Their hair is styled with beautiful swirling braids adorned with flowers and framing flawless faces. The women's hips sway seductively as their shining blue eyes land on us. Even though the wingless Valkyries are beautiful, these women make me feel inadequate, like our beauty is nothing in comparison.

Loki whispers in my ear, "These are some of the Vanir goddesses."

One particular goddess turns her head back to gaze at us. Loose strands of long blond hair brush over her face, momentarily covering her alluring blue eyes. Even the simple movement of her brushing the strand away is filled with sensuality, reminding me of my time with Freya and Freyr. Both the goddess and the god executed genteel, seductive movements, and both of them focused on love and fertility. However, Freya's dedication to her warriors, the angels of death, is a testament to their ability to partake in a war.

Curious eyes follow us as we pass through the

courtyard and city streets. By their reactions, many of them clearly recognize Loki in his current form, yet none approach to stop him. Surely, they know he's supposed to be confined within Odin's cells, which makes me wonder where their loyalties lie. Instead, the people of Vanaheim approach Elan and Tanda, bowing to the magnificent creatures and stroking their scales if given a chance. Many approach Britta to tickle Zildryss under his chin. The little dragon laps up the attention.

Britta swerves away from another hand reaching for her shoulder, where Zildryss lies, and faces Loki. "Why aren't they arresting you?"

"The Vanir have battles different from those of the Asgardians." Loki indicates the crowd, waving his fingers at a gorgeous goddess. "As you can see, they recognize me and are curious but don't do anything about it. I guess they don't listen to Odin, or perhaps they don't see me as a threat, like Asgardians do."

"What's the deal with everyone approaching the dragons?" I ask.

Elan lowers her head in friendship to another Vanir that approaches her and allows them to stroke her nose. *I don't think dragons are typical creatures on Vanaheim. I think they have heard of us and are curious.*

To seem friendly despite everyone fondling my

dragon, I smile at a god who's just run his hand over Elan's scales. "I guess that makes sense."

Britta's frown intensifies as another goddess reaches for Zildryss on her shoulder. "Shouldn't we be spending time gathering tears for Balder while passing all these gods and goddesses?"

Loki pauses and tilts his head to one side. "Not yet. You can't expect me to stay around for that, surely? I'm only here to help you find Idun. You'll have plenty of time after we find her." He spins and continues walking without waiting for a response.

We turn right onto another street, veering off the main path.

Loki's voice catches my attention. "Ah. Here she is."

A thin young woman with a basket looped on one arm stoops over an elderly goddess sitting among a group of people ahead. The young woman's long hip-length strawberry-blond hair falls over one shoulder, blocking the side of her face. When she straightens, the gathers of her light-blue dress sway around her ankles. Her hair falls back, revealing the material tapering around her thin waist, showing off her form up to her shoulders. She moves with grace, similar to that of the Vanir goddesses. Watching her is mesmerizing as she reaches into the basket over her arm and produces a piece of fruit much like an apple and hands it to the older woman. Delight passes over the older woman's face, and her hands wrap around Idun's hand holding the fruit. After thanking Idun, she eagerly takes a bite. As we move closer, the woman takes more bites, and I almost have to kick myself as the wrinkles on her face gradually fade.

Disbelief halts my footsteps. "That's just not right!"

Britta halts next to me. "Is the fruit that good, or is she eating it like this because of what it's doing to her body?"

Loki continues forward. "It's a bit of both."

"Have you eaten it?" I ask, picking up my pace to catch up with him.

He runs a hand over the sides of his face, accentuating the lack of wrinkles marring his features. "Can you not see how pure my face and body are? It's thanks to this fruit she's handing out. And like I said, it's probably the reason that Odin wants her to return to Asgard. Each piece of fruit the gods consume adds more and more years to their lives, and Idun is the only one who can supply the product." He pauses outside the group, and we stop. "After all, who doesn't want to live an extended life and look young and beautiful while doing it?"

I can't help noticing Idun is also thin and

extremely beautiful, and I wonder if she partakes in the fruit herself. She moves to the next person sitting in the group. Her long pale-blue dress flows softly around her ankles as she hands the fruit to the next person. Eagerly, the god takes the fruit, thanks her, and devours it. His wrinkles also disappear almost immediately.

"Idun," Loki calls just loudly enough for the woman to hear.

The woman turns, landing her pure-blue eyes on us before turning to Loki. Friendliness and compassion pour out of her, instantly putting me at ease.

Loki clears his throat. "These are a couple of Valkyries I know." He indicates us. "This is Kara, Britta, and their dragons, Elan, Tanda, and of course, Zildryss. Don't let his size deceive you." He eyes the little lilac dragon cautiously as through remembering the time he outed him in Alfheim.

"It's so nice to meet you." Idun curtsies then moves closer, her soft eyes studying us. "Are you after some of my fruit?" She runs a hand over Britta's cheek. "You don't need it. You are both still young and very beautiful. Although many start early."

Britta's cheeks turn bright red at the same time heat rises in mine. I'm not quite sure how to take that, since she deals with extravagantly beautiful goddesses all the time. But by Idun's expression, I think she means it.

I swallow and decide to accept the compliment. "Ah. Thank you." The tingling in my cheeks subsides. "We aren't here for your fruit. Odin has requested your presence." I study the others in the group of Vanir waiting for her fruit. "I'm sorry if this doesn't coincide with your plans, but we must take you back to Asgard."

She sighs loudly. "I guess if that's what makes the leader happy, then I should go." She weaves her strawberry-blond hair over one shoulder. "After all, he is the king of all the gods."

I can see she's unhappy about coming with us, and I spread my arms, hoping to appeal to her sensitivity. "I'd love to say that it's up to you, what you do, but I could really use your help in satisfying Odin. He can be so persistent and demanding at times. I hope you don't mind."

She weaves the basket over her other arm. "It's probably about time that I went back to Asgard anyway. I'm sure all the gods and goddesses there will be screaming for more of my fruit. Some haven't had it for a while and would be feeling the effects of aging."

She holds out a piece of fruit to Loki. "Would you

like some, Loki? You have a few wrinkles forming around your mouth."

Disappointment spreads over the mischievous god's face before he huffs and grabs the fruit to take a bite.

Idun cuts a sliver off one of her fruits, popping it into her mouth before cutting another slice and handing it to Britta. "Like I said, you don't need it yet, but would you like a taste?"

Britta's eyes light up before she shakes her head. "No. Thank you. I'm not sure that is wise."

Idun offers me a slice, piquing my curiosity. It looks incredibly tempting, and my control wavers as I reach for the fruit, but I pull back at the last second when caution niggles at my stomach. I shake my head. "Thank you, but no. I shouldn't. Although I have to admit it's enticing."

She smiles. "It is. It literally melts in your mouth, even though its texture is similar to an apple's." She places another piece in her mouth and groans with pleasure. Her face seems to lift emotionally even though I'm sure she doesn't need it physically.

Britta gapes at her. "Wow! I wouldn't believe it if I didn't see it. You didn't need to look younger, but I can see what it did to you internally after one bite."

I can also see what Britta means. Idun has been revitalized from the inside.

"Well." Loki interrupts our exhilaration. "I believe my work here is done. Catch you later!" A wry smile spreads over his face. "Or maybe you'll finally catch me." He morphs into another insect and flies off before I can stop him.

Chapter Seven

"**D**ammit!" I stamp my foot. "I needed to get a tear from him for Balder."

The goddess's blue eyes overflow with compassion. "It's such a shame about Balder." Idun's voice is crystal clear, so pure it rings in my ears. "Is that why you're here in Vanaheim?"

Britta nods. "Yes. Hel will only release him if we can get a tear from everyone on all the Yggdrasil realms, including Loki."

My eyes are fixed on the spot Loki disappeared from in insect form.

Idun places a hand on my forearm. "Don't worry about it now. He probably would have said that you needed to collect everyone else's before he'd shed a tear anyway. You know what he's like."

"Or he wouldn't have shed a tear anyway," Britta grumbled.

"Exactly!" Idun's voice is soft. She tugs on the

thin golden rope tied around her waist. Her pale skin shimmers in the sunlight as she fiddles with her basket. The fruit is almost radiant with the glow of Vanaheim.

Simply looking at the fruit makes my mouth water. Something is strongly alluring about the fruit.

The goddess raises her basket. "Are you sure you wouldn't like one?"

My fingers twitch, reaching for the fruit, before I pull them back. "No. Thank you. I think I should stay away. Although judging from your groan when you ate some, they seem extremely tasty." I frown. "Why is that?"

Her smile exposes her straight white teeth. "They're the fruit of life."

As I keep staring at the fruit, my resolve wavers, and my fingers extend toward it as though I'm mesmerized.

Something lands on my shoulder with a light thud, then Zildryss wraps himself around my neck several times. The little dragon presses his warm scales against my skin and drags his spinal fins, drawing my attention away from the fruit with the intentional discomfort. When he sees his efforts have worked, his tongue licks one eye then the other as he presses the soft part of his abdomen against my skin.

My vision is overpowered by images of gods

eating the fruit and all their wrinkles and age dropping away. Then he shows me how their lives seem to extend automatically for several more years. That doesn't seem bad until he finishes with images of this becoming addictive to the gods, and their addiction tampers with their mental health. The cravings turn my mouth dry. Trying to overcome its pull is like scaling an enormous mountain with icy peaks unless Idun gives them some more.

I peer down at Zildryss. "Is that really what the fruit has potential to do?"

His large eyes widen as he nods.

"Oh." Idun blinks her long eyelashes at Zildryss, and she tickles him under the chin. "I see you have a long-mouthed guardian. He probably knows what it does."

My mouth quirks. "He seems to. Can you confirm exactly what it does? I mean, Loki gave us a brief rundown, but I never completely believe him."

Idun retrieves a piece of fruit from her basket and turns it over in her hand. "It can bring back the beauty of youth and long life in most of the gods."

Britta gapes at the twirling fruit. "You mean it gives them a form of immortality?"

"Yes. It's almost immortality but not quite. It extends their life a great deal. The more they eat, the longer they live and keep their youthful looks."

I find that hard to process, though she acts like it's normal. "Isn't that breaking the rules of the universe?"

Her sweet smile widens, accentuating the missing wrinkle lines due to her consumption of the fruit, which has made all signs of aging vanish. "They are gods. Gods can break the rules as they wish. It's one of their perks." She offers the fruit to us again. "Are you sure you don't want some?"

"But we're not gods." Britta's eyes fix on the fruit, her body leaning forward eagerly.

"No. But you serve the gods, especially the gods of Asgard. And for that, you deserve a longer life." She holds out the fruit closer to us. "Here. Take it. You will find it will be the sweetest fruit you have tried, and I guarantee it'll have your mouth watering." She twirls a strand of hair around her forefinger and slowly lets it unravel as she pulls her finger free. "I'm only thinking of you and the life you deserve. The way you serve the gods will make you feel older than you should. They'll run you to the ground. This will help with that."

I snap my hand back to my side after noticing it creep forward toward the tempting fruit. "I'll pass. Thank you." I suddenly understand why this woman is so important to the Asir and Vanir gods... and why Odin wants her back on Asgard. He would treasure her for his wife. Odin would do anything for Frigg. I know I have to protect this woman and return her to Asgard in one peace. "The Valkyries already have long lives."

"This could make it even longer and keep you youthful throughout your entire existence," Idun says.

I smile, resisting the urge to feel for wrinkles on my face, unsure whether to take her suggestion as an offense. But then I remember I'm young, especially in Valkyrie terms. I have youthful skin and the promise of a long life if I don't die in battle. I straighten my shoulders. "Odin has requested your presence, and I must look after you until I return. I ask that you please come willingly." I can't help wondering why Odin is so desperate for her. He looks old in comparison to the other gods. But his wife looks very young and beautiful. That makes sense now that I know about the fruit. Perhaps he didn't marry a younger woman.

"Has Frigg taken your fruit, and is she waiting for you to return?" I ask.

"Frigg has taken much of my fruit. As for Odin, he has also taken this fruit."

"Then why does he look so old?" Britta asks.

Realizing that we're not going to take the fruit from her, Idun places it back into the basket.

"Because he has lived for many years longer than most gods. I guess he focusses more on the long life than the youthfulness. Looks aren't as important to him. Although in saying that, he looks much younger than someone his age. Every time he eats it, he loses a couple of wrinkles, but his life is extended, and that is what he is after the most."

Something about this whole extended life and youthfulness turns my stomach. It makes me feel that the gods are appalling creatures stuck in their own self-worth. Maybe I'm being too harsh.

"Have you decided to come willingly with us back to Asgard?" I try the friendlier approach even though I know I'll have to take her back anyway, whichever way she decides, or face Odin's punishment. It will be a lot easier if it's her choice.

She nods, her blond hair swaying. "I'll come with you. But first, I have many more here in Vanaheim that would like to partake of my fruit. I have spent much time on Asgard and think I should spend more time on Vanaheim. It is only fair."

"Okay. We have to see all the citizens in Vanaheim anyway. You can hand out your fruit as we work our way through the beings. Once we have all the tears offered, we'll take you back to Asgard."

She holds out a hand to me. "It is a deal."

Chapter Eight

We work our way through Vanaheim, approaching the different gods and goddesses. I have trouble keeping my eyes off the men wearing deep, plunging necklines exposing bare chests. The women are equally mesmerizing as they sway with grace, each movement appearing dainty and controlled. After seeing many Vanir, I understand how Freya and Freyr glow sensually. These are the gods and goddesses of fertility and love. The glowing golden hair on the Vanir makes the blond hair of the winged Valkyries seem drab in comparison.

As promised, Idun continues to travel through the realm with us, handing out her fruit to any of the Vanir longing for it.

A squeal of delight pulls my attention to the right. "Idun! Do you have some fruit for me?" A petite beautiful goddess charges toward us. Her swaying hips are hard to not ogle openly.

Now, I'm no human, and I don't find your beings attractive—disbelief taints Elan's voice—*but that goddess doesn't look like she needs any fruit. She actually seems too perfect.*

I place a hand on her leg. "I'd have to agree with you, Elan. I don't see anything that needs fixing, nor does she need to look younger."

Me either, Tanda adds. *I've studied each of the recipients, searching for signs of aging. I can't see any.*

Britta shakes her head. "They all seem perfect already, too beautiful and hardly a wrinkle among them. Yet each time they consume it in front of us, a radiant glow somehow accentuates their youth and beauty."

The squealing goddess takes the fruit Idun offers her and bites into the flesh. Even listening to the crunching sound makes my mouth water. The goddess groans. "This is so delicious, Idun." She takes another bite and struggles to chew the massive portion. She holds up a finger while her mouth works then speaks when the contents are gone. "Do you have another? My partner needs one. He's getting a few wrinkles around the corners of his eyes and is starting to look old."

Without waiting for an answer, she reaches into a

nearby group of people and pulls a young man from the mix. He looks flawless, and my eyes unintentionally rake over his bare chest and body, searching for the aging imperfections the goddess mentioned. I can't see a single wrinkle.

The young goddess lunges at the god and pulls at the corners of his eyes, pinching his skin and making lines appear on the outer edges. Deep red glows on the god's cheeks. "See? Just here. Can you see these deep lines that are starting to show?" She turns toward Idun, waiting for her response. "He desperately needs some of your fruit. I can't have him looking so old."

When she finally releases the man's face, I squint, trying to see the deep lines she's talking about. A two-year-old would have deeper lines. I shake my head to clear the fog of my disbelief.

Okay. Yep. These ones win the nutjob contest.

Hiding my face, I attempt to contain my laugh as I answer through our bond. *Oh, Elan. You're going to get me into trouble.*

Elan huffs. *I'm just telling the truth. The Vanir are vainer than any of the other gods, and that's hard to believe.*

Bearing an enthusiastic smile, Idun pulls out another piece of fruit and hands it to the god.

With my smile in check, I face the group again. *If I were this god, I'd be offended.*

The god takes the fruit from Idun. "Thank you so much. I would hate for her to think that I'm getting older. She may not want me anymore." Even his masculine voice has a golden ring to it.

Fire breath! Tanda exclaims. *I can't believe this guy. I would slap her around if my potential partner talked about me like that.*

"You must have read my mind, Tanda," Britta whispers. "That's exactly what I was thinking. There's nothing wrong with either of them. I didn't realize the Vanir were this ridiculous."

"Elan and I were just discussing that." I take a deep breath and sigh. "But we've got to let them do what they want to do. What do we know? We're just Valkyries and dragons. We just fight their wars and gather warriors for Valhalla. Although I haven't seen any other gods as vain as these. Perhaps it's a fertility thing. They are overly conscious of how they look."

"There's nothing wrong with that." Idun returns to our group, catching part of our conversation. "And that's what I'm here for. That's my service to these gods and goddesses. Eternal youth from the provision of my fruit."

We turn to leave when I realize I've forgotten to

grab any tears for Balder. I've been too distracted by the Vanir's weird behavior. I turn back and spot Britta already taking care of it. Her dedication to Balder being much stronger than mine, her focus is probably sturdier. In very little time, she gets the two in an emotional state, ready to cry over the simplest thing.

Britta only has to mention the name of the god of light to the goddess.

"He was so handsome!" she bawls.

I roll my eyes. That seems to be the primary reaction from most females.

But the god with her surprises me. "He was more handsome than I am," he wails. "What a tragedy!"

I shake my head in disbelief. She doesn't need my help to gather their tears. As I leave Britta with them, I overhear her say, "Thank you for your tears. This will go a long way to helping us get Balder released from Helheim. Please tell your friends to bring us their tears of grief, if they haven't already. We need every being to express how much they love him."

We trek farther into the city and find that the other gods and goddesses are much the same as the first couple. Each is extraordinarily vain and willing to cry for Balder without much coaxing. Every one of them declares how lovable and handsome he is.

Their exuberant praise is so intense that a sickness rises in my stomach. Balder's only a god. I didn't find anything extravagantly special about him. However, he was kind, so I would appreciate seeing him released from Hel's grasp.

After partaking of the fruit, one goddess approaches Elan with a streak of tears still down her cheek and runs her hand over the dragon's golden scales. Fascination fills her blue eyes before she turns to Tanda, only to receive a growl and a glower from the dragon, whose patience is running thin. Spotting the goddess's discomfort, Zildryss flies to her shoulder and circles her neck. The goddess giggles and tickles his back as he runs about.

"I think Zildryss likes being the center of attention." Britta smiles as she watches the little lilac dragon's progress. "Perhaps he should be the one grabbing the tears."

Leaning on one leg, I smile. "Perhaps, although I don't know how he would capture them. He would have trouble holding the vial."

We move farther down the street and climb the hill toward the city's peak. After charming the gods and goddesses in our wake, Zildryss joins us. With his help, we manage to catch a tear from every occupant in the city within a few hours. Many of them run up freely to offer their tears.

Scooping up another tear, I say, "Maybe this job will be easier than I thought."

Britta looks thoughtful. "It seems like it. I wonder how the others are doing in the different realms."

Stepping through the city gates, I assess the vast landscape to determine our next direction. "I hope they're getting the tears."

Elan lowers her golden eyes to my level. *I know this has been easier than expected, but you have to remember how much grief we received from other realms. I don't think they will all be as responsive, I'm sorry to say.*

I nod. "True. Not all of the realms are as welcoming as Vanaheim. I'm glad the feud between the Vanir and the Asir gods has been placed on hold, and they're willing to work together in this."

Chapter Nine

"What are you are doing?"

I investigate why Britta's voice is so high-pitched and find her swatting at Zildryss, who's circling her shoulders. He's clutching something in one talon and trying to stuff it into her ear.

I chuckle. "What are you doing, Zildryss?"

Idun giggles and adjusts the basket on her arm. "Awww. He's playing with Britta. How cute!"

We've traveled several leagues from the city. Tall trees line the path on both sides, and leaves crackle under our feet, often drowned out by the singing birds. Tanda's dark shadow passes overhead, giving me the comfort of knowing Elan is up there too. The dragons are scouting for the next sign of population, trying to speed our progress.

Britta grunts and swats at Zildryss again. When the movement pulls my attention back to the little dragon's antics, I notice faint music. It sounds like a fiddle, although I haven't heard one for many years. Automatically, it lures me away from Britta's protests. All distractions fade into the background as I move, my feet absentmindedly progressing one step at a time.

Vaguely, I register something scurrying around my shoulders. My right ear is plugged then my left in a matter of a second. The music disappears, and I'm stunned to see Zildryss holding my chin and looking into my eyes, his tongue lashing one of his eyes then the other.

"Zildryss!" I retract my head in shock at his sudden closeness. With my ears blocked, my voice seems to vibrate in my head. Turning to find Britta, I discover she's not behind me. I can't hear a thing, and I pull at one of the things shoved into my ears, only to have Zildryss scramble to press the item deeper. He stops in front of my face and shakes his head, his eyes serious.

It's a cute movement, and I laugh, reaching to pull the thing out of my ear again. The little dragon scrambles to my hand and shoves the plug deeper again. I swipe at him playfully, although his insistence is growing annoying.

Ignoring his silent protests, I tug at the thing he's placed in my ear and manage to pluck it free. "What are you doing, Zildryss?"

I twirl the item between my forefinger and thumb. It's fabric. Curious, I meet his stare, which holds strange desperation as he watches me intently.

"Why do you look so concerned, little guy? I don't need this in my ear." I can hear water trickling to my left, birds chirping, and the breeze whistling through branches and rustling leaves. "I'm missing out on all these beautiful nature sounds." I pull out the other plug, puzzled at the lilac dragon's continuing assessment. Shrugging it off, I toss the small pieces of fabric over my shoulder and search for the path.

Zildryss dives off, retrieves the scraps, and returns to my shoulder.

Britta's nowhere to be seen, and I seem to have strayed. "How did I get here?"

Zildryss holds up the pieces of fabric.

I shake my head. "No. I'm not putting those back in my ears, if that's what you're suggesting."

The little dragon sighs and curls around my shoulders, resting his head on his front talons, still clutching the fabric.

Slowly, I weave through the tree trunks until I emerge from the bushes onto the path.

Britta is waiting, leaning her back on a tree trunk. "Oh. Good. You're back."

Zildryss flies off my shoulder and into the forest

south of where we came out. After a few moments of squeaking and fluttering, he emerges from the forest. His movements are a flurry around Idun's head as he appears to be directing the confused goddess onto the path.

We fall into step and follow the path toward the sound of a waterfall, catching a glimpse when we round a corner.

"I don't know what happened. Do you?" I ask.

Idun and Britta shake their heads.

We follow the path along the river, all sounds drowned out by the cascading waterfall. The track weaves from the water's edge into the forest, eventually leading us back to the bubbling water winding its way through the rapids in the river. The water makes so much sound that hearing anything else is hard. If we were in a realm we knew to be dangerous, this would be disconcerting. Still, we revert to our training. Even though the realm is currently not our enemy, we remain on full alert for any movements and any potential ambush. Eventually, the sound of the water fades as the bubbling river widens.

"Zildryss, what are you doing?" Britta's steps wobble, bringing her into the center of the path. She swats at the tiny dragon in frustration and attempts to pull those pieces of fabric out of her ears.

Despite her effort, the lilac dragon isn't giving up.

I reach for him, but he dodges my grasp. "Zildryss. Perhaps you should show us—"

Loud thumps pull my attention away from the commotion as I search for potential danger. Another loud thump sounds, and my neck stiffens. I hope it's the dragons landing, but I reach for my bow from the quiver on my back and nock an arrow. With my knees bent, I'm ready for action and move forward.

Elan, is that you? I ask through our bond.

Never fear. It is us. Golden scales push through the trees, and her large form blocks the path.

Zildryss stops trying to block Britta's ears and flies to Elan's head, circling her horns.

I withdraw my arrow and slide it into the quiver. "Did you find any more villages?"

Tanda's head peers around Elan's massive form. Her glowing red eyes assess Britta as if looking for injuries. *Yes, we found some more villages not far ahead. Not as big as the last city, but there are plenty of people there.*

"Are we following the right path?" Britta asks.

Tanda's eyes soften when she sees that Britta is okay. *If you keep following this path, a fork ahead leads away from the river.*

The distant music of a fiddle drags my attention

away from the two dragons, and the urge to find the musician is too strong to resist. Something scurries around my shoulders, accompanied by high-pitched squeaks as things are shoved into my ears. My inability to hear the music causes my cheeks to burn with anger. Voices call to me, muffled by the plugs. It takes me a moment to realize that Elan is calling me. Strangely, I couldn't hear her before, even though she was communicating directly with my mind.

Angst lines her voice. *Where are you going, Kara?*

Blinking, I turn to find Britta following me, oblivious to Tanda's concerned gaze. Confusion fills the dragon's red eyes.

What are you lot up to? Elan asks.

Scanning the immediate area, I shake my head. "I don't know. I heard this music and found it irresistible. It's like it was calling to me, and I had to find the musician."

Elan snorts, and steam dampens my forehead. *We don't have time for this. We need to get the tears and get going. Loki is doing what he likes again, and that's not acceptable. Who knows what mischief he will get up to? Not only that, but we also have to finish this mission and take Idun to Asgard before Odin throws another tantrum.*

Shaking my head, I try to clear my thoughts. "You're right." I walk toward her while trying to remove the feeling fogging my mind. "I have no idea what I was doing."

It was like you were in a trance. Both you and Britta. This realm seems to be filled with very beautiful, dense people. It must be this strange realm. I'm guessing there is something here that makes people act that way. It's hard to believe that Freya turned out so well.

Remembering Freya's brother Freyr, I smiled. "I don't know. Freyr was a bit airy."

Elan nods. *True. But he was still more intelligent than this lot.*

I stroke Elan's nose, and something travels down my arm from the connection, clearing my mind, grounding my feet, and straightening my thoughts again. "Wow! I don't know what just happened, but I needed that."

Interesting! The scales on Elan's forehead bunch together in a frown. *Perhaps we should carry you and find the people that way. It's got to be quicker.*

Tanda grumbles. *I don't know why we weren't doing it before.*

Britta slips her hand under one of the red dragon's scales. "We were hoping to find more people in the forest. We thought Zildryss was telling us that someone is in here. There doesn't seem to be anyone, though."

Tanda nudges her playfully. *Except for whoever you*

think is playing that music. It's a bit hard to believe that you were hearing anything. I couldn't hear it. So you must be imagining things. She lowers her body. *Climb up. Let's go!*

Britta hooks a foot in the stirrup and hoists herself onto Tanda's hump. She grabs the reins, and the red dragon rises to stand.

Elan lowers to let me climb up. *I guess I'm going to carry Idun.* Her enormous body turns in a tight circle, swinging me around. *Odd.*

"What is?" I ask, distracted by Zildryss scurrying around Britta's shoulders and making high-pitched squeaking sounds.

Elan lifts her head, her golden eyes scanning the forest. *Where is Idun?* She spins some more, studying the trees. "I can't see her anywhere."

Each empty place we search turns my cheeks clammier. Both Britta and I have lost her, which is hard to believe.

Elan completes a couple more circles and sticks her head between some trunks before pulling out of the forest to check a larger open area. *She's nowhere in sight.*

- Chapter Ten -

Climbing off Elan's back, I search the area, shrouded in confusion. "Where has she gone?" I face Elan. "Was she here when you arrived? She was with us not long beforehand. But it's not like we're watching her every move. She's not our prisoner. She was coming of her own free will." My words are rushed, full of panic.

She was there behind you. But I didn't see her go. It was sudden. Her eyes cloud. *I think it was about the same time that you and Britta headed toward the forest in the direction of the water.*

Tanda stalks in front of us, her eyes trained toward the sound of the river. *That's when Zildryss started harassing you with the earplugs.* She turns to the little dragon. *Does that sound right to you?*

Zildryss nods, his eyes intense.

Oh, seriously! Elan slaps her tail against a tree's large trunk, and its leaves rustle loudly in the branches above. *Can't we go on any mission without a big drama? Now we've lost a goddess.*

"And one Odin wants us to return with. Maybe this is one of the failures the Norn was talking about," I add. "We need to find her, or else I'm going to be in deeper trouble, if what Ratatoskr says is true."

Elan slashes her tail through the brush. *Oh. I couldn't care less what Odin thinks. He's never going to be happy. I just care about the goddess. Idun seems nice.*

While I stare deep into the forest, something lands on my shoulders, and I jump but relax when I see it's Zildryss. His warm scales press against my neck, instantly filling my mind with his communicating visions. He shows me the back of Idun as she wanders trancelike in the other direction. Britta follows not far behind her until Zildryss lands on her shoulders and stuffs fabric in her ears. The little dragon's actions stopped Britta from following the music, leaving Idun to continue through the forest in her trance.

The depth of Idun's trance disturbs me. The mesmerizing tune draws her away unwaveringly. The vision gives me an understanding of what happened to us when we lost track of time.

Petting the lilac dragon's head, I ask, "Are you sure this is what happened to her?"

The tiny dragon circles my shoulders to the front and nods, his big eyes wide.

"Do you mean to say that this music mesmerized us, purposely dragging us away?" I ask.

The dragon nods again.

I stare straight into his big eyes. "So you're saying that when you shoved stuff into our ears, it stopped us from hearing the music and therefore stopped us from following the music?"

Zildryss nods again, his tongue slashing from one eye to the other.

Britta calls down to us from the hump on Tanda's back. "Does he know where Idun is?"

Zildryss pushes off my shoulder and wraps himself up against Britta's neck. In seconds, understanding flashes across the Valkyrie's face.

"Oh," she says. "You were so busy trying to stop us from disappearing that you didn't have time to block her ears also."

Zildryss scurries around Britta's neck to face her, and he nods before holding up two pieces of fabric as though asking if he can shove them back into her ears.

She screws up her face. "Is that really necessary?"

He nods.

Contemplation crosses Britta's face. "If that's what happened to Idun, then in order to find her, one of us needs to be able to hear the music. Only a female like a goddess or Valkyrie can hear the music in a mesmerizing way. Is that correct?"

He nods and lashes his tongue from one eye to the other again.

I frown. "What about you, Zildryss? You seem to know that the music is playing. Can't you hear it?"

Zildryss presses his stomach against Britta's neck again and, moments later, understanding fills her eyes. "He can feel the vibrations of the magic woven into the music. He can't hear the music or the direction it comes from." Gently, she pushes Zildryss and his fabric away. "Then I should be the one without plugs, directing you to the player. Go and stick those in Kara's ears, and let me be the bait."

Standing next to Tanda, I look up at her. "No, Britta. I'm not going to let you be the one in a trance. With the dragons around, surely we can both be drawn by the music."

She shakes her head. "I don't think that's a good idea. One of us should be able to think straight in case we need to use magic to get Idun." She rubs Zildryss under the chin. "I trust you lot to stop me if I'm lured too far into danger. So it's going to be me."

I open my mouth to speak.

She holds up a finger and points at me with a glare. "No arguments."

Huffing, I cross my arms over my chest. "I guess so. It's not like you've given me a choice." I focus on the little dragon still sitting on her shoulders and plant a stony scowl on him. "Zildryss, don't you dare let her be consumed by this. I expect you to block her ears before she's in the grasp of whatever it is."

The little dragon stands on his back legs, straightens his face with responsibility, and salutes me like a soldier.

My heart melts. "Do you know what is luring us?"

The little dragon nods enthusiastically.

"Okay." I hold out my hand. "Do you still have the fabric for my ears?"

He dives off Britta's shoulder, lands on my arm, and drops the fabric into my palm. His eyes narrow at me.

Don't worry. Elan nudges the little dragon with her nose. *Both Tanda and I will help Kara ensure Britta is stopped in time. We didn't hear the music.*

I take comfort in knowing our dragon friends are here and push the pieces of fabric into my ears and watch Britta's face for any evidence of change. "Do you hear the music?"

She shakes her head.

Tanda huffs. *You'll be able to tell when she hears the*

music. You two were like zombies when you took off after it.

Both Britta and I head farther down the path, tracing our footsteps backward. As if on cue, when we reach the part where we last heard the music, Britta goes stiff-necked, her face blank and her eyes wide. Trancelike, she turns off the path and into the forest, heading toward the river. Slowly, she weaves through the tree trunks, and I follow within viewing distance. Zildryss splays across the back of my head, his front talons reaching to cover my ears. He feels like a dead weight hanging from my hair, but I know he's making sure my hearing is blocked.

I glance back at the dragons. Their heads are lowered as they attempt to weave through the trees. Watching them trying to maneuver their enormous bodies in a small space is almost comical. But at the same time, I worry that they won't get to us via land in time to help if they have to. At least Zildryss can remain with me, his trusty pieces of fabric ready to shove into Britta's ears as a backup.

I return my attention to Britta to assess her progress, but she's gone. Panic lodges its spear into my heart. I have to find her. I promised to protect her. I can't lose her like this. Quickening my pace, I search frantically for her black Valkyrie uniform and long brown hair.

Elan's groan echoes in my head. *Argh! We're going to hit the sky. We can't get through these trees. We're too big.*

Continuing to search the trees, I answer through our bond. *Okay. Keep an eye out for Britta. I lost sight of her.*

Seriously? Oh, Tanda's going to be annoyed.

It's not my fault. I turned around briefly to see what was taking you two so long. When I turned back, she was gone. I check over my shoulder to catch a final glimpse of the dragons. I can barely see them between the large tree trunks in the distance.

Elan sighs. *I get it. These things happen quickly. We will break down the trees to help find her if we have to.*

No. Not unless it is necessary. I don't think the Vanir gods would appreciate our destroying their forest. Let's hope I find her, or maybe you'll be able to see her from the sky.

- Chapter Eleven -

Leaves and twigs billow toward me, pushing their way through the tree trunks from the force of the dragons' wings as they take to the sky. The wind whips a strand of my black hair over my eyes, and I pull it away. All I can see are trees, endless numbers of trees. With my ears blocked, I can't hear any noises Britta might be making while trekking through the dried leaves and twigs on the forest floor. Using sight alone will make finding her difficult.

After pacing several hundred feet in the direction I hope she disappeared, I still don't find any trace of her. Zildryss whacks me twice on my shoulder with his tail then jabs the tip slightly to the left. Hurrying, I catch a glimpse of Britta's brown hair glowing briefly in a patch of sunlight up ahead. My heart quickens.

"Good job, Zildryss!"

Breaking into a jog, I charge toward Britta, zigzagging through the trees before she disappears again.

"Britta!" I call.

She continues as though she doesn't hear me. I call again, only to receive the same lack of response. After trying to get her attention several more times, I truly understand what the dragons were saying. When being entranced by the music, we were cut off from everything around us.

Britta's pace is surprisingly quick for someone who isn't in her right mind. She easily weaves around branches and rocks in her path, even though her body is rigid.

My attention is fixed on Britta, and I'm determined not to lose her, when I stumble over a large root. Zildryss takes flight as I fall and circles my head, hovering over me until I scramble to my feet and dust myself off. His little talons pitter-patter on my shoulders by the time I take my first step to catch up to the disappearing Valkyrie. The distance between us has grown, and fear churns in my stomach over how close I am to losing her. The back of her black uniform is only barely visible through the shadows of the trees. It's not the easiest color to find in the shadows of the forest.

Another stream of sunshine beams between the trees and catches on Britta's brown hair. She's gotten farther than I expected. I run, this time also paying attention to the ground and the obstacles waiting to hinder me.

"Don't let her get out of your sight, Zildryss."

The little dragon stands at attention on my shoulders, eyes fixed on the entranced Valkyrie.

"I hope our sacrifices pay off, and the music will lead Britta to Idun. If that isn't what took her, we are in deep dragon dung."

Zildryss wraps his tail around my neck, and I'm surprised to feel comfort from the touch. Still, my heart settles only when we're within a couple of yards of Britta, the beat slowing to a more normal pace. I want to grab my friend, but something tells me I shouldn't touch her. I don't know whether the feeling came from Zildryss or if it's just my gut having its say. I would hate to break the link to the music and make Britta lose all connection. That could ruin our chances of finding Idun.

I start when Elan's voice enters my head. *Have you found Idun yet?*

Glancing down, I narrowly miss tripping over a rock. *No. I'm having a hard-enough time keeping up with Britta.*

Tanda and I have spotted a new village, although we haven't seen the goddess yet. Are you still with Britta?

Yes. I suck in a deep breath. *She isn't making it easy to follow her. I hope she's heading in the same direction that Idun is.*

That's great! You're still with her. I'll let Tanda know. Don't lose her. It will be impossible for us to find her in that forest. We only catch glimpses of her brown hair in the sunlight now and then. The trees are too thick to see anything. Although there is water nearby in the form of a lake.

I wonder if that's where Britta is heading, I muse.

That's odd.

I swipe some branches away from the path and push through. *What is?*

There's this little weaselly-looking man thing sitting on a rock in the middle of the lake. And he looks like he's playing some kind of instrument. Although I can see him move, I can't hear anything. Pfft. It's like he's miming it.

It is odd. Why would anyone sit in the middle of a lake and pretend to play an instrument?

Wait! Elan pauses, keeping me mentally on edge. *I've just seen Idun. She's walking into the water, straight toward the little weird guy playing the instrument. I wish I knew what the guy is playing that has her attention.*

I brace against a trunk when a root hooks my boot. Do

you mean you can't understand because you can't hear anything?

Yup! I can't hear anything. Hang on. She looks to be in a trance, just like you two were. The scrawny man's arm is working overtime on that instrument.

Glimpses of water shine through the trees. That's where Britta is heading. I quicken my pace until I'm almost marching with her. I'm sure my footsteps aren't silent. Leaves and twigs should be crunching under my feet, yet Britta doesn't react to my noise. Seeing the Valkyrie unobservant and unready to fight whatever may come her way is weird. We've traveled quite some distance, which makes me ponder how strong the music must be to lure us all this way.

After only a few more paces, Britta bursts through the edges of the forest, into the open area around the lake. I remain out of sight, within the tree line. Instantly, I catch sight of the little man Elan told me about. His scrawny body is scrunched into a squatting position. A fiddle is cocked under his chin as he slides the bow back and forth over the strings.

Idun's strawberry-blond hair glimmers in the sunlight, her legs thigh-deep in the water. Her dreamy eyes are fixed on the unusual man. He's so skinny that he seems to be missing muscles. Long dark locks of matted and patchy hair flow over his shoulders. The man has harsh features, a pointed nose and a jutting chin. His skin is pale and lackluster. He looks starved, yet he has the full attention of the beautiful goddess, Idun, and the attractive brown-haired Valkyrie.

He rocks from side to side, his arm working the bow quickly over the strings. I'm thankful my ears remain plugged, disabling me from hearing his music, which seems to be aimed toward females and not dragons. His long, bony legs folded underneath himself, he perches on a rock, wearing not much more than a loincloth. I can't see anything attractive about him. Even his skin is wrinkled from weather and age.

Idun glances away momentarily, allowing me a chance to catch a glimpse of her face. Her eyes are blank, her face emotionless, and she seems to look straight past me. The man's hands work faster, and she turns back to him as though nothing exists in the world besides him.

She treads deeper into the water, swaying as though dancing through its resistance. Her basket drapes over one arm, swinging with the movement of her arms as she swirls and twirls. Her attraction to this man she doesn't know is odd and doesn't make sense. He looks creepy and strange, almost like a giant goblin. The goddess is beautiful in many ways and has the tools to extend the lives and youth of others. She should surely be attracted to someone better than this seedy guy.

Elan, can you call her? I don't want to do it in case it attracts the little man's attention.

Oh, I have already been trying, and so has Tanda. She keeps ignoring us. Suddenly, she yells directly into my brain, *Idun!*

I jump. *Thanks for the warning.*

You're welcome! Just proving my point that she should have heard me.

She sounds like she's smiling cheekily, and I search the sky for her, but she must be invisible.

Idun! Elan screeches again, literally shaking my insides with her loudness.

Idun's movements don't even register the call. She would never ignore that call if she were in her right mind.

Idun! Tanda's voice fills my head with a higher-pitched shout, yet the goddess doesn't respond.

I groan. "This is ridiculous," I say to myself more than anyone else.

I look for other ways to grab her attention. Apparently, I'm going to have to go into the water with her, which will alert the little man. Even Zildryss would be detected outside of the trees. I'm not sure how deep the water is. If it's over our heads, dragging a screaming Idun back to the shoreline will be a mission.

Frustrated by the lack of options, I call, "Idun!"

Even though I've screamed her name, she doesn't even blink. However, I did catch another's attention. The man playing the fiddle turns his eyes toward me and grins, exposing disgusting brown teeth. I cringe.

Chapter Twelve

My heartbeat quickens while my mind whirls for the next best move.

As though she's reading my thoughts, Elan's voice fills my head. *Dragon scales! I saw that. That's just creepy.*

You're telling me! I'm grateful for the fabric plugs in my ears. If they weren't, I'm sure I wouldn't have seen his smile for what it is. *Idun is fascinated with him.* I screw up my nose. *I can't for the life of me see why.*

Yeah, I know. I'm not even your species, and I can tell he's grotesque.

Idun wades deeper into the water.

I'm going to grab her, Elan says. She's still invisible, but a gusty breeze gives away her movements.

A few moments after Idun's head disappears under the water, the water around where she disappeared thrashes with waves, yet the goddess doesn't emerge again.

Dragon scales! I didn't get her.

Suddenly, a streak of red circles above us. *Britta! What are you doing?* Panic laces Tanda's voice. I pull my eyes away from the goddess to see Britta enter the water, still in a trance, heading toward the ugly man with the fiddle.

Zildryss launches off my shoulder and lands on Britta's, wasting no time while shoving the pieces of fabric into the Valkyrie's ears. Britta stops almost instantly just as Tanda is preparing to dive down to grab her. The Valkyrie shakes her head as though trying to shake off a sense of haziness. Her body arches forward, and her hands rise high as she realizes she's surrounded by waist-deep water.

Looking puzzled, she peers over her shoulder and spots me on the shore. Her mouth moves, but the plugs in my ears prohibit me from hearing her.

I lift my hands in a questioning gesture then indicate for Britta to return to the shore, and as she does, Zildryss holds his talons over her ears as an extra precaution, scowling over his shoulder at the man on the lake. Relief floods through me when she reaches the shore. At least we were able to save her from whatever the strange little man was about to do to her and Idun. The thought of the goddess reminds me that she is also in peril. Moments later, the dripping-wet Idun is lowered onto the shore by an invisible force.

Elan turns visible, standing over the drenched goddess. *I had a few more tries. She was sinking fast.* Water trickles off the golden dragon's scales.

Releasing a sigh of relief, I mutter, "Thank you, Elan."

But Elan doesn't hang around for any praise. Instead, she takes to the sky and flies straight toward the man with the fiddle. His arm works the bow rapidly, already capturing Idun's attention.

Argh! Tanda groans. *I'm going to break that instrument. It's getting on my nerves, and I can't even hear it.*

Elan grabs the little man from his rock and unceremoniously dumps him on the ground in front of us. Disturbing shivers run up my spine as his beady eyes land on me. Seemingly undeterred by the enormous dragon, he raises his fiddle to his shoulder and drags his bow across the strings.

Elan whips her tail, knocking the fiddle from his grasp and sending it flying several feet away. Surprisingly, the clattering instrument doesn't break as it skims over the riverbed stones.

The arrogance leaves the little man's face, washed away by sorrow. For a moment, I almost feel sorry for him as he scrambles to his feet. The sympathy diminishes when he scurries across the ground to retrieve his instrument, his spindly arms outstretched. In only a few more steps, the instrument will be in his arms again.

Elan pounds along the shore and stomps a large front foot directly between the man and his fiddle. *Oh, no, you don't.* She lowers her head, narrows her eyes, and exposes her extensive array of sharp teeth. Even my legs want to shake with fear at the glare, and I know she's friendly.

The man scurries backward, moving more quickly when she expels a malicious laugh.

Elan growls, holding her ground. *That's it, little guy. Back off.*

The man stumbles over his feet then regains his balance. He manages to find the strength to stand straight and smile. "I was only going to grab my fiddle." He shrugs, his posture nonchalant. "It's just an instrument. I love to play, you see." He indicates Idun, sitting on the shoreline with saturated clothing, looking puzzled over how she got there. "As you can see, the ladies love it."

Britta moves closer to Tanda, pressing against her leg for protection.

Elan moves closer to the little man, her head lowered, and exposes her teeth further. *Oh, I know what that fiddle does. I've seen it with my own eyes. Don't you for a second think that you have us fooled. I know what normal behavior for these young ladies is. How they acted when you played was not normal.* She snorts out a large plume of steam.

The little man wipes sweat from his forehead then face, and he holds up his hands, trying to make Elan pause. "I meant no harm. It's only a little music, and I love to entertain my lady friends." He straightens his back proudly.

Zildryss makes a funny sound, catching my attention, and the little dragon shakes his head in disapproval.

One side of my mouth rises. "It appears that Zildryss has a different opinion. Would you like to share it with us, Zildryss?"

Zildryss wriggles his backside and weaves around Britta's neck, settling next to her skin.

Her face turns blank, and recognition lights up her features after a few moments. "He's called a fossegrim. And from what Zildryss has shown me, he lurks in the waters with his fiddle, ready to prey on any passing women. He lures them with the music, brainwashing them to come to his side. His tunes enchant the women, and they will do anything to be by his side. Once there, they are fixated, unable to move until they starve to death." A visible shiver runs down her spine, and she looks at the fossegrim, horrified. "He is not to be trusted. He will not let them go unless somebody comes to rescue them. This is rare because not many people know about him or his kind."

The fossegrim shakes his head, the sparse strands of hair brushing his shoulders. "That's not true. I'm friendly and love to entertain the ladies." He spreads his arms wide in a display of honesty. "It's not my fault that they love my company so much that they stay by my side. It's not like I restrain them in any way."

Britta places her hands on her hips. "But you do. There is magic in your music that binds us to you, controlling us and making us believe you are the most handsome man in the world. Your music tricks us into thinking that you are the only thing that matters, making us sit by your side." She holds out the pieces of fabric that used to be in her ears. "If it weren't for Zildryss and our dragon companions, the three of us women would have been slaves, mentally chained by your side. We don't even remember what happened to us when we were under your music's influence. So don't you give us that rubbish that it was only music."

Having dried slightly, the goddess still appears lost.

I ask, "Is that what you felt, too, Idun?"

Idun wraps her long, wet blond hair around her neck and drapes it over one shoulder, allowing it to fall in front. She fiddles with the ends momentarily before looking up and nods. "Yes. It's a strange feeling, as though I didn't belong to myself, and I was so fixated on him." She grabs her basket of fruit from the ground as though it can bring her comfort and screws up her nose as she takes him in. "I haven't felt anything like it before." She toys with her basket. "Now that I think of it, I have heard of him. I didn't know that he lived in Vanaheim. He must be the reason so many women have disappeared in this area."

Idun picks up one of her pieces of fruit and rolls it in her fingers. "Many of the gods were telling me about it when I was handing out the fruit earlier." She looks at the water, and her face turns somber. "I wouldn't be surprised if there are many bones buried in this water—the skeletons of many women dragged into the deep after not eating or sleeping for so long, fixated by the music's spell."

Elan approaches the lake's edge. *I shall have a look.* She strides into the water until it reaches her knees then sticks her head beneath the surface. The seconds seem like hours as the anticipation of what she might find eats away at my stomach.

As she slowly returns to the shoreline, the suspense is killing me. "Well?"

Yes. There are many skeletons down there. And I'm guessing they're all females. There are so many that the water is not that deep. She glances down and peers through the water's surface. *I can see them from here. The water is crystal clear. I didn't realize this before, as I didn't know what I was looking at, and the water reflects the sky and clouds. It's disgusting, especially when I can feel the older, decaying ones snap under my feet.* She screws up her snout. *On the other hand, there are some with flesh still stuck to the bones.* She glowers at the fossegrim, approaching him with her teeth bared. *Maybe I should eat him.*

- Chapter Thirteen -

E lan stands menacingly over the fossegrim, growling through her teeth and snorting bursts of steam. The weaselly man backs away, tripping over a rock, and lands on his backside before attempting to crawl backward on all fours.

"Wait, Elan," I call begrudgingly.

Elan casts me a side-glance yet doesn't pull away from stalking the fossegrim.

The little man nods enthusiastically. "Yes. Yes. Wait. I don't taste good. I guarantee it."

Elan growls. *I wasn't going to eat you for your taste. I was going to eat you because you threatened my Valkyrie and her friends.* She towers over him farther. *Nobody threatens my rider and her friends.*

"I apologize." The fossegrim holds up his hands. "I didn't mean to offend you or your friend." His chuckle is laced with uneasiness. "Perhaps there is something I can do in return to ask for your forgiveness." His voice wavers, and his eyes plead with me.

I hold out a vial. "Actually, there is one thing. We need a tear for Balder. He came to an untimely demise and died out of battle. This saddens us, and we want to give him a second chance to die an honorable death. But Hel won't release him unless everyone sheds a tear for him."

He wipes away the sweat gathered on his arms and shoulders from Elan's hot breath combined with his fear and slowly sidesteps around the massive dragon. "You want tears? I'll give you tears."

I hold out a finger. "I don't just need tears. They need to be genuine and for Balder."

"If I give you my tears for the wonderful god of light, will you excuse me for what I did?"

"Kind of. I will call Elan off, and this time, she will listen." I cast Elan a warning look. "And we will let you go. But I will do this in the hope that you won't kill any more young maidens as well."

Apprehension crosses the fossegrim's face. "But I need to play my music. I live for my music."

Noticing his indecision and desperate for everyone's tears for Balder, I add, "We will be putting up a warning sign and spreading the word through Vanaheim to be wary of you and where you are situated. You will not be allowed to play your music loudly, nor are you allowed to play near the boundaries that we set, in order to lure the young maidens to follow you to your lake."

He shows no hesitation. "Agreed." His face saddens, and his footsteps quicken as he dodges past Elan and heads toward me, the golden dragon stalking him not far behind. "You can have my tears. Not a problem." He throws back his head and wails. "I'm so sorry that Balder was taken from us too early. It saddens me that such a wonderful god has passed like this. I miss him. He was my only genuine competition for the beautiful maidens." He wipes his nose with his arm. "If he's not around, then I will have to fight them off." Tears trickle down his cheeks.

Stunned at the mini rivers flowing down his face, I hold out the vial and catch them. "You have a lot of tears for Balder."

He grabs my wrist. "Yes. I do. The extra tears are from the young maidens that lie on the bottom of this lake. They are the ones that left Balder to follow my music in hopes of finding a more handsome man." He wipes away a trail of snot with his bare arm, making me grimace. "Each one of them would have wept for Balder and would miss him dearly if they heard that he has been taken too soon. Even though they chose me over him. I'm happy to express their tears for the lesser man."

"Okay." I screw up my face and pull back. "I'm glad to hear that you can express the dead women's tears as well. Perhaps you should also cry for their souls, seeing as you left them to die at the bottom of the lake."

When he finally finishes crying, I cover the vial and put it away safely in the pack stored on Elan's saddle. "Thank you for your tears. We appreciate your help. But we'll still warn the maidens nearby about what you are capable of."

The fossegrim shrugs then moves away from the dragons. "As long as the dragons let me live, I'm happy." Something in his tone makes me wonder what he's thinking.

Elan plonks down on her backside next to me. *I think he's overconfident that the music he plays on his fiddle will bypass any warnings.*

Not wanting the fossegrim to hear, I respond through our bond, *I think you're right, Elan. We can do nothing else other than warn the women and tell them to cover their ears when they travel in this vicinity. But this deal has been struck, and I won't go back on the agreement. At least we got more tears for Balder.*

After spotting Tanda breathing hot air over Britta to dry her soaked uniform, Elan does the same for Idun. The goddess's clothes are fixed to her body, and goose bumps rise on her arms.

Half crawling, half walking, the fossegrim collects his fiddle and bow and drags them with him as he sludges through the water back to his rock in the middle of the lake.

I call across the water, "Don't play that fiddle until we leave."

He shrugs. "Of course, of course. I wouldn't dream of playing the fiddle while you are still here." His grin holds an innocence that doesn't sit right with me. "I have to play the fiddle, though. It brings me peace and sanity."

"So you said," I mutter.

Elan pauses from drying out the goddess. *If you play it before we leave, I promise I will eat you.*

Tanda stands at the side of the lake. *And if she doesn't, I definitely will. But I will make it last, and you will wish that it were Elan instead.*

The little man holds up his hands. "Relax. I promise I'll wait until I think you're out of reach." He poises himself on the rock with his elbows resting on his knees, and he props the fiddle under his chin with the bow in one hand.

Even though he hasn't played anything yet, he's not instilling any trust in me. Not wanting to watch my dragon eat a being, I quickly climb onto Elan and pull Idun up. "Let's go, Elan."

She lunges into the sky, followed by Tanda with

Britta on her back. The dragons fly us out of earshot, with the wind blowing in the opposite direction, helping to carry any music away and finally allowing me to relax. I relish in the sound of the cool breeze thrumming against my eardrums. If he does play the fiddle, we won't hear it.

The breeze changes direction, and my hair whips across my face. I tie it back and admire the beauty of Vanaheim. Luscious green pastures line the unusual landscape decorated with beautiful crystal-clear springs and animals of all kinds.

Elan's wings rise and fall, lulling me into peaceful security. Knowing that my beautiful dragon friend is with me and carrying me fills me with warmth and reminds me that she will always have my back, a feeling I will never grow tired of. She's a friend who will protect me from all adversity and any dangerous creatures that come my way.

We pass over a couple of villages, but the dragons continue flying for a little while before circling back to the next village in line, almost as though they're giving us some rest before we continue hunting for tears.

We circle the village and a plain near the forest. Something catches my eye, and I peer downward. An animal that looks like a white stag grazes below. But only one horn protrudes from its forehead instead of a broad set. It looks like a unicorn, but the body is more like a deer than a horse. It's unlike any animal I've seen. On top of its unusualness, its coat glows dully, reminding me of Balder. The animal almost seems to be a tribute to the god of light. The thought softens my heart. Animals may not be able to cry, but this one shows sympathy in another way.

Chapter Fourteen

Getting tears for Balder doesn't prove difficult. The god of light and joy is loved by most of Vanaheim for his handsomeness and his heart. The people of the realm also like that he glows, radiating beauty similar to that of Vanaheim. Because of their willingness, completing the realm takes very little time and speeds my escort of Idun to Odin in Asgard.

Tanda and Elan fly close to each other, carrying Britta, Zildryss, Idun, and me back to Yggdrasil.

Britta hooks a windswept lock of hair behind her ear. "Do you think Loki is back in Asgard? He still hasn't sworn to cry for Balder."

I shake my head. "As per usual, the god of mischief is making me work to get him to do anything." I sigh loudly. "I wish I knew what his intentions are. One minute, he seems to be on our side—the next, he's not. If he was behind Balder's death, then he's going to make me work hard to get a tear from him. It would have been nice if he'd just cried when we saw him earlier. But no, he has to make us chase him."

I wriggle in the saddle to find a more comfortable position. "To think that in the early days, he was once one of my best friends in a different form. Now, I have no idea what he's planning. Since that final battle in Asgard, I never know exactly what he's going to do next. It's almost as though he uses our past fake friendship to manipulate me and to avoid what he should be doing."

After soaking up the beauty of the shining lands of Vanaheim, Elan circles and lands in front of Yggdrasil. Idun flips a leg over Elan's large back, and I help her lower to the ground before sliding off my beautiful golden dragon.

Tanda lands near Elan, and Britta slides over the large hump and jumps to the ground with Zildryss wrapped around her shoulders.

Britta faces away from the World Tree, her hands on her hips. "It will be kind of sad to leave this realm. It's so pretty. It's a shame to think we have to go, but I want to see Balder back."

Moving next to her, I place a hand on her shoulder. "Don't forget: we have to make sure Loki has returned to his cell and try to find out what he is up to. And we need to make sure that his children aren't stirring up mischief. The Midgard serpent is still free, and I'm not sure I trust what Hel says. She may be planning or executing attacks yet denying it."

Britta screws up her nose. "Why can't they just live peacefully?" Sadness fills her eyes. "We have to see how the others are doing with collecting tears for Balder. I have this horrible feeling that it's not going to be enough."

"Haven't you got that right?" A nasal voice cuts through our peace and rubs against my nerves. When I turn, Ratatoskr is sitting in the branches of Yggdrasil, unsurprisingly. "From what I see, you've been a complete failure."

Glaring up at him, I ask, "And how do you figure that?"

"Oh, please. Where do I start? You haven't even taken Idun to Odin yet. He demands that you leave right this moment."

I gasp in disbelief. "We've been gathering tears to get his son back."

"Well, Odin isn't happy. He says you're the most unreliable Valkyrie there is. He should never have let you and the wingless ones be rewarded and acknowledged as proper Valkyries. He said he should redefine your position and put you lot back into servitude."

My blood boils, and I say through my teeth, "Well, then, Odin has unrealistic expectations. We're already doing one mission for him, and he expects us to drop everything just to bring back a person who can make his wife look younger and live longer." I throw my arms out to the sides. "It's ridiculous. We're supposed to worry about the ones that matter more than looks and a long life."

Ratatoskr dusts his claws on his white chest then peers at them as though checking their shininess. "Well, I'm just passing on the message. You know me —I'm just the messenger. Although I have to agree. You have been pretty slack. You didn't even get Loki to cry for Balder."

Britta flicks her hands at Ratatoskr. "Argh. Why did we take so long to use our new magic on him?" She straightens her back and somehow looks superior to him even though she's below the branch. "Loki promised to cry for him later. We are going to find Loki as soon as we get back to Asgard and get that tear from him." Her words are distinct and sharp, challenging him to dispute it.

Ratatoskr waves a paw at us, and his mouth

moves, yet nothing comes out. He holds a hand over his throat and tries again. Nothing happens. He frowns, looking puzzled at why no words are coming out.

Britta laughs. "Oh, I wish we'd had this gift earlier. It's so satisfying, seeing this rude little rodent unable to talk."

I watch the squirrel attempt to speak and find the humorous side. It is liberating to shut the messenger up.

Realizing what's happening, Ratatoskr stomps his feet and frantically waves his paws. When Britta doesn't pull the quieting spell off him, he puts his paws on his hips and huffs. The breath hisses from his nose, but Britta doesn't remove the spell. We laugh some more. The squirrel indicates dramatically toward me then Idun before enthusiastically shaking his head.

"Britta, I hate to say this, but it's probably best to let him speak, just in case he is saying something important."

Britta's shoulders sag with disappointment. "I guess." She waves a hand at the squirrel.

Ratatoskr holds a paw to his throat and clears it. "As I was trying to say, I don't care if you're successful are not. I'm just the messenger. Besides, you haven't even got this one here to cry for Balder." He waves a claw at Idun.

"Ratatoskr!" Even though Idun's voice is clear and sweet, it also holds a reprimand. "I will cry right now for Balder. The Valkyries haven't asked yet. I don't blame them. They have been rather busy since I have joined their group. But it is certainly not a matter of my refusing. He was one of my favorite gods." Her beautiful face distorts with grief, and a tear runs down her face. I don't even have to get my bag. Idun fishes into it and pulls out the vial, catching the tears accumulated on her face. Every movement she makes shows her genuine grief for the god of light.

My heart softens almost to a breaking point as I observe her emotion. She looks distraught, and I'm grateful she's helping us. She wipes her face with a sleeve and returns the vial to the bag. "There. Done. I didn't need to think twice." She shakes a finger at the squirrel. "And you are rather nasty to these Valkyries."

Ratatoskr shrugs. "That's what I do." He moves to leave then pauses. "But just to let you know, all the tears collected are useless at the moment." He feigns a pout. "I hate to break it to you. Your friend Hildr has failed to get one to cry. One of the giants of Jotunheim won't cry."

"What is she doing in Jotunheim?" Britta asks. "She was supposed to be in Midgard."

"Hildr finished Midgard and decided to help with the land of the giants." A wry smile creeps onto Ratatoskr's face. "Just because you got Vanaheim to cooperate, don't think for a second that your mission has succeeded." He struts toward the trunk. "I'm sure, even if you return Idun, Odin will be annoyed because the Valkyries haven't achieved what they should. The way you're going, Balder will never be released." He smiles sweetly over one shoulder. "And remember: I'm just the messenger. These are not my words." He stops just before the entrance to Yggdrasil and straightens his back. "I almost forgot. Do you have a message to return to Odin? Or are you sick of trying to send insults to the king of the gods?"

Idun places her hands on her hips, her basket swinging from an arm. "Now, you tell that king of gods that he is one rude god. Tell him that if he wishes my services, he is to treat them better. These Valkyries have done a lot for him and Asgard." She moves closer to Ratatoskr, and the red squirrel places one foot in the hole, ready to leave. "I won't be coming back to Asgard straight away. He can wait for my services, whether it be for him or someone else." She shakes the basket of fruit in Ratatoskr's direction. "I'm going to take this basket with me, and I'm going to travel with these kind Valkyries. Perhaps I can help." She waves a dismissive hand at him. "Now, run along and disappear."

Ratatoskr looks taken aback momentarily and shakes his head. "Geez. These Valkyries have really brainwashed you."

Idun hisses at him.

Ratatoskr holds up his hands. "I just meant you don't usually defy Odin like that. But I will be the messenger and pass on your message to the king of gods. I hope he doesn't take it too personally." He cups his hand over his mouth as though about to tell her a secret. "You know how that can turn out." He scurries into the hole and disappears.

I study Idun with wonder. "Thank you. I'm so sick of dealing with that rodent. Nothing I do seems to please Odin, and I have to hear it from the squirrel all the time. It's nice to have someone else defend me."

Dimples I didn't notice before form in her cheeks when she smiles. "You're more than welcome. Odin should treat you better. After all the things you've done for Asgard, I can't believe he still treats you like this." She shakes her head. "It's unbelievable!"

Elan lowers to the ground and waits for me to get up. *That's the way he is and has been since we started communicating with him.*

"That's right." I help Idun onto Elan's back. "I was hoping to go back to Asgard, but we do need all the tears for Balder. Somehow, we were given the easier realm this time. It's time to do some more challenging work."

- Chapter Fifteen -

I dun standing up to Ratatoskr for us was a relief. It has always seemed like we're in a losing battle against Ratatoskr and Odin. I don't know what the goddess will be able to do to help us gather tears for Balder, but I'm willing to give her a chance.

Elan shoots through the hole into Yggdrasil. *I must say I like what Britta did to Ratatoskr back there. It was nice to have him shut up for a change, especially against his will.* She cackles down our bond, which warms my heart.

I laugh with her. *It was a nice change, wasn't it?*

Soon, Elan shoots out of the trunk into the icy realm of Jotunheim and lands not far from Yggdrasil. The frosty air in the land of the ice giants numbs my face and hands. Magnificent frostbitten mountains and frozen lakes spread far and wide. Tanda lands next to Elan, her red eyes scanning the landscape for potential danger.

Britta rubs her upper arms. "It's rather fitting that we're back in the birthplace of Loki's monster children to chase down a giantess that won't shed a tear for Balder, especially seeing as it may have been Loki who helped kill him in the first place."

I tug at the edges of my dragon-scale cloak in an attempt to block out the icy wind. "Don't forget that Loki's mistress also lives in this realm."

Britta pushes her lips to one side. "And to think that it's Loki's children who are causing all these hassles, and it was Loki who managed to discover what hadn't sworn to not hurt Balder."

Tanda lands her red eyes on Britta. *And it was most likely Loki who guided Hodr's blind aim straight at his brother's heart to kill the lovable god.*

Rubbing my upper arms to get the blood circulating, I say, "When you say it like that, it seems as though this is all preplanned, that we're walking into a trap. Not necessarily a trap," I add, correcting myself. "More like walking into an impossible assignment."

Idun places her hands on my shoulders. "I will give you as much help as I can. Balder was one of my favorite gods. He was never arrogant, and he was always kind. Not that all gods are arrogant, but many are conceited and think they are the only thing that matters. That can be tiresome."

Britta's eyes are sincere when she looks at the goddess. "Thank you. We need all the help we can get. I admired him from afar and up close." She grins. "I long to get him back. Not that he was really mine."

Idun tuts. "Honey, everybody liked Balder, whether they admitted to it or not." The goddess looks pointedly at me.

I pull on Elan's reins. "I don't know what you're talking about."

Idun shakes her head, her long locks cascading around her like a waterfall. "We all liked him up close and even from a distance. It's a shame he had a wife."

In an attempt to ignore the conversation, I slip a hand under one of Elan's scales and tune into her vision. Her sight is different from mine, with fewer colors, but the range of her vision is a lot longer. *Can you see the others, Elan? Are you able to hear them or call them?*

Her eyes scan the horizon, and she paces, circling and taking in the entire three hundred sixty degrees before shaking her head. *I can't see them. I'll try to call them.*

Thank you.

A couple of minutes pass as we wait to see if the others reply to Elan. I pull the hood of my dragon-scale cloak over my head and shiver as I wait for warmth to be trapped within. Even though the cloak is wrapped around me, air seeps out through the split made when we were in Helheim. The cloak received a bashing as we were escaping evildoers and supporting Sleipnir while trying to lift him over a boulder using my cloak. Memories of the evil we experienced there send nightmarish shivers down my spine, and I wonder how Thor is doing in the under-realms. I'm not in any hurry to return to any of those places and potentially face again the attacks we endured. Fighting off those evildoers was the worst battle I've faced. We were surrounded by darkness and thick fog, and it was hard to see anything, and their intentions were far from pure. They were actually quite sick.

Needing to focus on the dangers of this realm, I push the distressing thoughts away. The threats we've faced here aren't to be dismissed lightly. Even the dragons faced peril at the hands of the giants.

That's probably the reason Thor sent the warriors here instead of one or two Valkyries, and it's most likely the reason Hildr decided to join them after she finished on Midgard. She's always ready to fight.

Something white moves in the distance. I thread my hand under Elan's scales again and connect with her dragon sight. Creatures covered in white fluff move freely over the hills. We came across them last time we were here, and they have proven aggressive although not as bad as the frost giants on a rampage.

Idun shivers, and I shift, moving to sit behind her and wrap my cloak around both of us. The goddess is petite, making it easier to cover her also.

Elan's voice cuts through my thoughts. *I can hear Drogon. They are several leagues away, off to the right. It's difficult to hear his response. They are fine and are getting several of the giants to cry. But it's true—there is one giant who won't weep. They plan on going back to her later. First, we must find them and see if we can aid them in any way.*

Tanda, carrying Britta, follows Elan when she takes off.

"Wow! That's amazing!" Idun coos. "It's like I'm floating on air, except I can't see myself either."

I notice that Elan has turned invisible, giving the goddess the front-seat experience of being invisible because she is wrapped in my cloak.

Tanda swoops before angling her body to fly higher to use the clouds as cover. I scan the area below, looking for Hildr, Drogon, and the einherjar. In moments, we see them as the flight of the dragons carries us quickly across the land.

Hildr is standing in front of a giant with Drogon by her side and the warriors circling the three. They look tiny compared to the giant, yet he isn't threatening them. Instead, he sits on a boulder with his chin propped on a palm and an elbow resting on his knee. He looks as though he's listening to a story.

As we approach, I realize that he's one of the giants who captured us on our last trip to the realm. Seeing him sitting passively on a boulder, seemingly fixated on what Hildr says, is strange. The einherjar wait in the background, ready to attack if the giant's mood changes for the worse.

Tanda? Elan calls. *We've spotted them. We're going to stay out of sight in case it disturbs the mission.*

Are they okay? Tanda asks.

They seem fine. But we're not sure what they're doing. Elan descends, taking us to just above the giant's head. *I'm going to circle for a while to assess the situation.*

The giant seems to be fixated on Hildr.

If he's felt my breeze, he's not letting on. Elan dips and swerves, swooping low.

A warrior carries a large vial toward the god. The giant's face distorts with emotional pain, and a large tear trickles down his cheek. Two einherjar are needed to carry the large vial to catch the teardrops. Their knees buckle slightly under the weight as they struggle to hold it steady. Beads of sweat pearl on the warriors' foreheads despite the coolness of the air as they march toward Yggdrasil, the vial held between them.

Hildr bows to the giant. "Thank you. We appreciate your tears for Balder."

With sunken shoulders, the giant rises to his feet and walks away, every footstep showing signs of profound sadness.

Remaining invisible, Elan lands next to Drogon, waiting for the giant to leave before turning visible.

The warriors struggle under the weight of the tear as they walk in the opposite direction.

"How many of those have you collected?" I ask.

Hildr turns to face me, unsurprised. "Quite a few, actually. And they are so heavy. I'm glad the einherjar are the ones responsible for carrying them. I could carry some with my magic but not all of them."

I brush Idun's hair out of my vision to keep it from tickling my face in the breeze. "Can we help?"

Hildr studies Idun, assessing the goddess. "Possibly. I believe there are only a couple more giants to collect tears from. One of them is refusing to cry." Worry bunches her freckles together. "If I don't get them to cry, then our whole mission has failed." She nods at Idun. "Who's this?"

"This is Idun. She is a goddess Odin wants me to take back to Asgard. Her fruit gives the gods a longer life and youth. I should've taken her back already, but she wanted to come."

"This is a perilous place for a goddess," Hildr says.

Idun smiles. "I understand. Hopefully, I can help."

Hildr levers herself up onto Drogon's back by a stirrup and grunts. "Hope so. But we'll see. They're a different breed here."

- Chapter Sixteen -

We follow Hildr through Jotunheim to collect tears from the remaining frost giants. Seeing the giants showing emotion is a strange sight, after my last couple of times in the realm. I can't help checking over my shoulder for any danger they may bring, and I cringe deeply every time thunderous footsteps make the ground vibrate as the giants come and go. Each giant sheds a tear, and watching the strong warriors carry them away is almost comical.

Hildr pulls a list from her pocket and ticks off another giant. "If this is correct, there's just one more to go. And she's the most stubborn of them all. I've already tried her a couple of times, and she has refused to cry." She turns to Britta and to me. "Perhaps you lot can get her to cry. I certainly can't. I would try the violent approach or force her by magic, but unfortunately, we need tears of genuine grief, not tears of pain."

Britta straightens on her saddle. "Lead the way, Hildr, and we'll follow. I'll certainly give it my best shot."

Hildr grasps Drogon's reins tightly and leads us over ice-tipped mountains and skims through frozen valleys. Even though we need the warriors' help to carry the tears once caught, we save our energy by flying and waiting for the einherjar to cross the land. When I dismount Elan to stretch my legs, my feet slip and slide on the ice, and I almost topple to the ground. As I pace around Elan, I clasp her golden scales to secure my footing.

Idun leans against Elan's enormous form, her basket of fruit still looped over an arm. "Here they come."

The scene is intimidating, even though they're our allies. So many warriors making their way across the land together gives the impression that they're here for war. We know they're here for our protection, but some frost giants may have seen it differently since the remaining einherjar are only a few, compared to how many arrived on the scene at first. Many have left Jotunheim to carry away the giant tears. I couldn't imagine that seeing so many warriors would help relax this final giant and coax her into crying for Balder. About thirty warriors remain and file through the valley, marching over the snow. A couple of warriors slip on the ice and slide partially down the hill.

Britta clasps Tanda's reins more tightly. "I'm so glad that I didn't have to cross that. It looks rather tedious."

A couple more warriors slide to their backsides, and their comrades assist them down the hill.

Idun smiles sweetly at each warrior who passes. "Asgard thanks you for your service."

Those simple words plus a smile from a pretty goddess instantly brighten the warriors' moods.

Hildr stands between two large boulders, facing the group. "The cave entrance isn't far away. It's through this gap. The passage from this place is too narrow, and we have to leave the dragons behind."

Drogon snorts out a large plume of steam then lowers his head close to his rider. *I don't like you going in there again, Hildr. It makes me nervous when I can't see you.*

Hildr grabs one of the horns under his chin and shakes it playfully. "I know you worry about me. I'll be fine. At least this time, I have Kara and Britta with me as well as the warriors."

Drogon's intense gaze fixes on Hildr as she turns to leave.

As I pass between the boulders to follow Hildr with Idun by my side, Elan tilts her head and peers through the crack after me. *I don't like you going in there either.* She attempts to poke her nose through the slit. *I don't understand how a giant can get in there if dragons can't.*

Hildr plays with the hilt of her sword. "I believe there's another entrance for the giants, but I haven't found it." She shrugs. "It's the only explanation I can come up with."

Let me see. Tanda nudges her head into the spot Elan was only moments before, her red eyes filled with concern as she assesses the area and watches Britta join us. *Yeah. I don't like it either.* She blinks then pulls back. *At least take Zildryss with you. He may be small, but he is a dragon and has some surprising uses.*

Without being asked, Zildryss chirps, making excited noises as he swoops down from the top of a boulder and lands on Idun's shoulder.

Hildr scratches him under the chin as she talks to the three large dragons. "Don't worry. She wasn't worried about attacking us the last time I visited her. She just refused to shed a tear for Balder."

Drogon pushes to the front of the group. *I know. But I still don't like it. She has been known to attack before. The first time, it took all the einherjar to get you out of there safely.*

Hildr steps through the thin passage and places a hand on Drogon's brown nose. "That time, I think the number of einherjar we took made her panic. I don't blame her. Perhaps she thought she was under attack." She rubs his nose in circles. "The last time I went, she was calmer. We are taking fewer warriors this time. Hopefully, that'll calm her more."

The warriors' boots clop on the stones and hard ice as they follow Hildr through the narrow passage toward the cave.

Hildr surveys the entrance then each of our faces, her chest rising as she inhales deeply. "Let's do this."

I nod. "Let's hope that, between us, we can extract the final tear for Jotunheim."

Zildryss darts onto Hildr's shoulder and wraps his body around her neck.

The redheaded Valkyrie runs the backs of her fingers over his spinal spikes. "Hey, little guy. Are you going to help us?"

The little dragon nods.

Hildr smiles. "It's always a pleasure to have your company." She picks up a stick from our side of the tight passage and holds it out to Drogon, who lights it with his fiery breath.

This cave reminds me of the one where we found Angrboda, except this one is situated in the colder parts of Jotunheim. Perhaps many of the caves on Jotunheim look similar. I'm not in a rush to find out.

Darkness closes in as we go deeper into the cave.

Hildr takes some flame onto her hand and gives the torch to Idun. Britta and I also secure part of the flame and hold it on our hands, creating more light for the group.

A cold breeze pushes us from behind, chilling me to the bone, even through my dragon-scale cloak. I pull it tighter around my body, attempting to close the rip in the back. I eye the others with pity. They don't have a big cloak like mine and must be freezing. An even colder breeze pushes my hair over my face, and I brush the dark strands away. The wind changes direction, oddly blowing from the front, leading me to think that Hildr must be correct in assuming there's another entrance to the cave somewhere. After a while, we come across a large opening in the cave ceiling exposing the snow-capped mountains. The breeze coming from a different direction suddenly makes sense. A large boulder sits in the center of the open-skyed area, and we fork around the edges then rejoin as a group on the other side.

Hildr's footsteps falter. "She's not here. She has always been in this area when we have come before."

Idun holds up her torch, exposing more cave ahead. "Perhaps she has gone deeper into the cave."

Hildr's eyes show apprehension as she spins and

looks back at where we came from. "The cave gets smaller the farther we go in."

All of us turn to face the entrance of the cave.

Idun stretches the torch upward, exposing a ceiling so high that it barely shows in the torchlight. "How big is this giant?" Her voice sounds high-pitched and nervous.

"This big." The overly loud voice cuts through the cave's silence.

With wide eyes, the four of us spin to face the direction the voice came from. The giantess is huge. Her blue-skinned face and hands seem to glow in the torchlight, and I wonder how we didn't see her before. Patched animal hides are sewn into a long-sleeved tunic and leggings ending in moccasins to protect her feet. She approaches us, her footsteps almost silent, and I understand why we didn't hear her coming.

"Thokk." Hildr almost chokes on the word. "You startled us."

The giantess leans forward, her long, straight blond hair falling over the sides of her face. "That's what I do to beings that shouldn't be here in my cave." She scrutinizes us with her gaze. "Who are these different beings? Are they here for my dinner? I'm getting hungry, and I eat trespassers."

Idun stumbles back from the giantess and trips

over a rock, her strawberry-blond hair flying in all directions as she scurries to regain her balance. The torch scatters over the floor, extinguishing at a warrior's feet, and her basket of fruit empties over the ground. It's a clumsy movement for the goddess of youth and longevity. I drop back toward the goddess, share my light with her, and help her pick up her fruit.

Her cheeks flush, and she smiles. "Thanks. I guess I got a bit of a shock. It wasn't what I was expecting."

"I can hear, you know." Thokk's voice is powerful, radiating energy through the cavity and making the hairs on the back of my neck stand up. The giantess's eyes land on Hildr. "You. I have already given you my answer."

Hildr's shoulders stiffen, and defeat momentarily niggles her features. Zildryss circles her neck, and she straightens her shoulders. "I know what you said. These are my friends. They come in peace. Perhaps you will hear them out."

Turning her back to us, Thokk hunches and moves farther into the cave, entering another open area with a fire burning in the center. Apprehensively, Hildr follows, and we walk behind. The giantess sits on a large rock beside the fire and pulls her animal-hide tunic over her knees. Her large blue eyes observe us with coldness as we near, slashing my hopes that she might shed a tear for Balder.

As we haven't been told to leave, we enter and stand not far from her, while the warriors wait just outside the room.

Instead of telling us to go, she stretches her legs, warming the bottoms of her feet against the fire, and something about the way she moves reminds me of someone, but I can't place who.

"I didn't invite you here, and I told you not to come back. I despise it when I'm not listened to." She lands her cold gaze on Hildr, and threatening malice laces her tone. "I should eat you."

Chapter Seventeen

The giantess climbs to her feet and towers over us threateningly. Her shoulders stoop to fit under the cave's ceiling. "What do you think? I think I have a right to eat you, don't you?"

Hildr takes a deep breath, her hands clenched by her side. "We have been through this before. Yes, you did tell me not to come."

"Then what are you doing here?" Thokk thumps the cave wall, and shards of rock topple around us.

Hildr's knuckles turn white as she clenches her fists tighter. I stand next to her, hoping my presence will help calm her frustration.

Hildr whispers through her teeth. "Perhaps I should just hit her with some painful magic to make her cry." She circles one hand to gather her magic.

I shake my head. "You know that's not the kind of tear that will work. And good luck trying to make her cry from physically inflicted pain. She's huge."

Hilda smiles slyly as she studies the giantess's feet and notices a toe protruding from her moccasin. "I don't know. Perhaps a sword under a toenail would do wonders."

I grimace at the thought. It would be rather painful. "There must be a better way."

Britta shifts to stand on Hildr's other side. "Let me try."

Hildr moves aside. "Be my guest."

Hesitantly, Britta approaches Thokk. Zildryss wraps himself around her shoulders as if to motivate her. The Valkyrie straightens her back, a new sense of encouragement seeming to wash over her. She clears her throat. "So, Thokk, have you heard of Balder?"

The giantess crosses her arms over her chest. "I've heard of the god. The other Valkyrie there"—she points an enormous stubby finger at Hildr—"has informed me about him. All gods are the same, if you ask me."

"Not quite." Britta glances at Hildr then back at Thokk, a dreamy expression filling her face. "Did Hildr tell you about how wonderful he was? How pure of heart and how friendly and caring and just he was?"

Thokk screws up her nose. "Yes. I've heard."

The Valkyrie clasps her hands together and rests them under her chin. "And have you also heard that he was tremendously handsome? And did you know that his skin glowed, holding an aura of light?"

The giantess crosses her arms tightly. "I don't care for your kind and your so-called beauty." Her blond hair falls over her eyes, concealing a face more homely than attractive. "Just like you lot probably don't think any of us are attractive." She brushes her hair behind her ear. "Among frost giants, I'm considered quite attractive, but you probably don't see it." Her eyes are accusatory as they focus on Britta before scrutinizing Hildr and me.

Britta swallows, struggling with a smile. After a couple of moments, she says, "Beauty is in the eye of the beholder. I agree with you there."

Inwardly, I cheer her diplomatic answer, glad I'm not the one trying to remark on her beauty.

The giantess's blue skin glows dimly in the firelight, and she leans back against the cave wall, seemingly unmoved.

Noticing this, Britta says, "If you aren't worried about the beauty of our kind, then perhaps you'll consider thinking about the god and his kindness?"

Thokk straightens her legs, warming the soles of her feet against the fire. "As I said, I don't care for any of your gods. They are blank, unfulfilled individuals." She raises a shoulder in a half shrug. "I don't care that they were attractive in your eyes, nor do I care if this god was a nice person. He has nothing to do with me. Everyone should die when they should die. Their time is up, no matter how they died, honorable or dishonorable according to Asgard's beliefs." Thokk waves a dismissive hand at us. "Now, run along, little Valkyries. Leave me alone, and don't come back. Or I will eat you."

Britta's shoulders slump as she turns to leave, disappointment and failure spreading through her eyes.

Hooking my arm in Britta's, I head with her toward the entrance, our footfalls on the rocks sounding empty.

Hildr joins us, her sadness making Britta's disappointment seem mild. "Thanks for trying." She walks silently beside us, eventually exhaling a pained breath. "I don't mean to put a damper on your effort, but basically, our mission has failed. We haven't been able to get a tear from every being, and now Hel won't release Balder. I think we deserve his release from our effort, although her agreement was that it must be a tear from everyone. I can't believe I'm part of the failure. It's just like the Norn predicted."

She sounds close to tears, and I turn to study her just as her footsteps falter and her shoulders sag with disappointment.

I catch her arm then pull her in line with us and

hook my elbow through hers. "It wasn't just on your watch. It was ours also. We came to help, and we didn't succeed either."

Britta moves to Hildr's other side. "What Kara says is correct. I really hoped we could help, only we didn't. Now, I feel like it's my responsibility that Hel won't release Balder back into the living world, giving him the chance of an honorable death. He is brave and mighty and should be one of the warriors for Valhalla." Tears run down Britta's face, and she captures some in a vial before packing it away to add to the collection for Hel. Her grief runs deep, and I find it a little over the top because of her infatuation with the god of light. Still, I understand how much of a waste his death was.

Zildryss wraps himself around Britta's neck, and the Valkyrie strokes his tiny head, relishing his compassion.

"I know, little guy," Britta says. "I really tried. I did. It's a shame you don't have any magical powers that can convince stubborn giants to listen."

Even the tiny dragon's face is anxious, filled with a sadness he can't hide.

When we reach the edge of the cave before the open cavity in the ceiling, I search for Idun. "I should get you—" I lose track of the thought when I can't find her. "Where's Idun?"

Hildr and Britta shrug.

"I thought she was following us." I turn to look back, and my stomach twists in knots when I spot the goddess standing defiantly in front of the giantess.

Britta gulps. "I hope she's not doing anything stupid."

Chapter Eighteen

"What is she doing?" I can't contain my dread.

Thokk's eyes flick toward me then back to Idun, a scowl rising on her face like an approaching storm. "Weren't you leaving with the Valkyries?"

Curiosity gets the better of me, and I discreetly move closer to see what the goddess is doing.

Idun smiles sweetly up at the giantess. "Perhaps I can entice you with another sort of taste."

Somehow, the giant's scowl deepens, yet judging by the goddess's broadening smile, she isn't put off. "I am Idun. Have you heard of me?"

Thokk grunts. "No. Why would I?"

The goddess shifts her basket in front of her, letting it catch the giantess's eye. "I provide the gods and goddesses with these fruits."

The giantess screws up her nose. "So?"

"These fruits hold the gift of prolonged life and

youth. You won't find this fruit anywhere else, and it's a special privilege to receive it. Getting older and facing the end of life disturbs many. It doesn't give immortality, although it certainly gives the partaker a much longer life and youth."

Thokk crosses her arms, still towering over Idun. "Get on with it, goddess. What are you trying to get at?"

"Well, normally, these are only reserved for the gods and goddesses. However, if you're interested, I can make a deal with you."

When Thokk just scowls more, Idun continues, "I will share these delicious fruits with you for the rest of your life if you're willing to shed a tear for Balder's sake." She dips one of her elegant hands into the basket, pulls out a plump, juicy fruit, and holds it up for the giantess to see. "It seems like a decent bargain, don't you think?"

Thokk straightens her back and crosses her arms tightly over her chest. "What makes you think I want any part of that? That is absolute nonsense. Do you think a giantess like me would want to take part in that sort of behavior? We are confident women who don't need to rely on the power of vanity. Besides, our beauty outweighs any beauty of you Asir and Vanir."

Idun takes a couple of steps back, lowering the

fruit she's holding out. Shock and disbelief cross her face, for she clearly doesn't know how to receive this information. "I thought all beings wished to live longer and remain young and beautiful."

Thokk sneers. "That's how little you know about us giants. We don't care about external appearances or 'extended life and beauty.'" She makes air quotes. "That's a lot of vain hogwash, something completely unnecessary." She screws up her nose. "So fake and disgusting." The giantess pushes up to stand, hunches over Idun, and points at the door from where we came. "Now, leave before I squash you." She lifts one giant foot and holds it over the sweet goddess.

I run forward, my hand in a stopping motion, and push Idun from under the foot. "Now, there's no need for that." I stand in front of the goddess. "I'm sure she didn't mean any harm. Idun was only trying to see if she could find something that would entice you to shed a tear for Balder. In her defense, most gods and goddesses would fall over backward for some of her fruit. It's because of this I've been ordered to bring her back." I smile sweetly. "In one piece, of course. Odin wants her to return to Asgard as soon as possible, and he would take it as a threat if you were to eat her. We were sidetracked by coming here to see if there is anything that you may want, to entice you to shed a tear for Balder."

Thokk stomps, her foot narrowly missing us. "Do you think I care what Odin wants or sees as a threat? There's nothing you can give me that would be worth my tear to be shed for Balder. I have absolutely no interest in shedding one for him, and nothing can convince me otherwise." Towering over us, she points at the door again. "Now, leave!"

Knowing we've lost this one, I drag the goddess toward the entrance of the cave. Footsteps thump behind us, turning my cheeks clammy when I spot the giantess following us, slowed only by the lowering ceiling and tightening walls. I yank Idun faster, struggling to get her out of the giant's reach. Thokk seems to have lost her patience with us and is determined to punish us for our efforts.

Despite our haste to remove ourselves, Idun still manages to look disheartened. "There must be something she wants, something she'd exchange for a genuine tear for Balder."

Still dragging her toward the entrance, I shake my head. "Sadly, nothing comes to mind, and the pursuing giantess is making it difficult to concentrate."

The thundering footsteps become softer and sparser as we progress farther from Thokk. Turning, I can see her in the distance, her face barely visible in the darkness. I call back, "We're leaving now. Please remember that if anything changes your mind and you're willing to shed a tear for Balder, let us know, and we will come and collect it. That's all we ask. We weren't trying to cause mischief."

Thokk squats on the spot, her giant stomach pouching toward the ground, her powerful voice reaching us easily. "I don't care." She flicks one hand in a dismissive gesture.

We don't argue anymore, realizing it's pointless and most likely counterproductive. Disappointment wracks us as we exit the cave, the cold wind snuffing out the remaining palm flames as we return to the dragons and warriors waiting for us.

How did you do? Elan searches our faces. *Not that good, huh?* She works out the answer before we reach the edge of the cave.

I shake my head. "No. I've failed Balder, failed Thor, failed Odin..."

Drogon snorts, and a blast of snow spreads and turns to water before hitting our skin. *What happened this time? You all look awful.* He claws at the ground. *Did she hurt you?*

Hildr shakes her head. "We aren't hurt. This time, we have definitely lost. Unless a miracle takes place and strikes some empathy into the giantess, Balder will be stuck in Helheim. It doesn't matter how many other tears we manage to gather. We failed this mission."

Drogon eyes all our faces. *Did everyone fail?*

Hildr rests her forehead against the hard brown scales of his leg. "Yes. Unfortunately, everybody gave it a go, and everyone failed. She just refuses to cry."

Tanda's red eyes glow with compassion as she fixes them on Britta. *I'm so sorry. I can see this has upset you.*

Perhaps it's for the best, Drogon says.

When Hilda gives him a strange look, he shrugs, spreading his wings wide with the hooks at the folds pointing up. *You said it yourself. Helheim doesn't seem that bad. It's not as nice as an honorable death, but at least it's not a terrible place. And for some reason, Hel seems to like Balder.*

Hildr momentarily stands dumbstruck before understanding flashes across her features. "And it's true. Even so, we really tried to achieve this. Most of the realms worked with us willingly, even most of the frost giants."

Britta nods. "A lot of beings cooperated and shed a tear for the god of light, even many that classify us as their enemies. So far, everyone has cooperated except this giantess. But we have done everything we can. If we have collected everyone else's tears, perhaps Hel will have mercy and write off the one failure. Surely, what we have collected is much better than most would have done, and it's definitely better than not trying."

I find myself nodding. My soul clings to the last fragment of hope that remains. I can never quite push away a tiny glimmer of hope that Hel may overlook one being's lack of tears. In my last attempt to collect Thokk's tear, I ask, "Can anyone think of anything that may make the giantess change her mind?"

"Sadly, I'm all out of answers and ideas." Hildr's hand twitches over her sword, a habit she hasn't quite gotten over, even after years of being a warrior. As though realizing what she is doing, she yanks her fingers away from the hilt.

"At least we have one thing Odin has requested," I say, looking at Idun. "I get to take you back to Asgard. It isn't everything he wants, but hopefully, that'll be enough, and he will be thankful."

"Ha!" Hildr climbs onto Drogon's back. "Like that's going to happen."

I climb onto Elan's back and help Idun up the dragon's side and onto the saddle.

Elan nudges my leg with her mouth. *Well, it's going to have to do. There is nothing else you can do, and besides, when does Odin have to prove himself by doing the hard work?*

"Um. Have you forgotten that he's a god?" I ask. "Not just *a* god, but the king of gods."

Elan harrumphs. *Like that means anything other than it's gone to his head.*

A strange sound gurgles up from my belly. I want to laugh and cry at the same time. Despite my trying to hinder them, tears of compassion well in my eyes over our failure and Balder's demise. My tears fall past my dragon and onto the ground.

Britta scoops up a tear and gives it to the warriors.

Chapter Nineteen

In an attempt to push away my sadness and desperation over a failed mission, I search for something I can achieve soon. Facing Idun, I say, "Let's get you to Odin. Then we'll see where we can go from there."

Idun wraps her arms around my waist as she sits on the saddle behind me, and Elan takes to the sky. Cool air brushes my cheeks, numbing my face and causing my skin to match my emotions over our failure. Despite Thokk being adamant over not shedding tears, there surely must be some way to get her to do it. But my hopes diminish with each beat of Elan's wings.

Following are Drogon with Hildr on his back, Tanda carrying Britta, and Zildryss wrapped around Britta's shoulder. The icy land of Jotunheim passes beneath us, and we reach Yggdrasil in only an hour or so. When Elan ducks through the large hole in the trunk, I know I won't miss this realm. It's so cold and uninviting. At least this time, the giants left us alone to collect tears rather than attack us, as they did the last time we came.

After only a few moments in the trunk, we arrive at Asgard, and I relish the familiar sight of the stone pillars and harsh, rocky land of the gods of the Asir. The view brings me comfort. The rugged rocks are beautiful in the dry, desolate land lit by the early morning sun. I've lost count of how many days I've been away, and dread fills me over the thought of telling Odin we failed. I don't know if I can convince him that hope still exists when I'm not even sure myself. Idun's basket of fruit whacks my hip, reminding me that I'm also bringing good news to the leader of the gods.

The dragons circle Odin's palace, alerting Birger and Gorm of our arrival. The guards' broad smiles take up most of what shows of their faces under their large horned helmets. While Gorm keeps patrolling the palace door, Birger's quick footsteps drum down the expansive steps.

The instant Elan lands, Birger stops in front of her and strokes her nose. "Lovely to see you again, my friend."

And you. Elan nudges him with her nose. *Although I don't believe we have time to play hide-and-seek today.*

His smile widens, seeming to make his large nose bigger. "I'm always willing to play, if you change your mind."

This is a far cry from how the two guards used to treat wingless Valkyries and dragons. Both were used in demeaning ways, and I smile at the change in attitude. This is one of my successes, and I realize I need to give myself more credit and not take Odin's harsh words to heart.

Birger's helmet strap slips off his small chin, and he hooks it back under, indicating the palace door. "Odin will be happy to see the goddess of longevity. He is expecting you and is waiting in his hall."

I attempt to swallow the lump growing in my throat then remind myself again of my successes and pull back my shoulders.

Birger interacts with Drogon and Tanda as the Valkyries and Idun climb off the dragons' backs.

"Good to see you back." Gorm snaps his ankles together and juts out his prominent chin as we reach the top of the stairs.

"Good to see you keeping well, Gorm. How come you have to stay at the doors?" I ask, remembering the times both Gorm and Birger have played with the dragons in the courtyard.

Gorm frowns, though all I see under his large helmet is the bridge of his nose wrinkling. "Odin is getting twitchy. Fenrir is still wrestling with his restraints, and other creatures from Helheim have surfaced on Asgard."

I scowl. "That's odd. Hel said she wasn't worried about Loki being imprisoned and that she wouldn't be attacking Asgard." I leave out the part where she said he can readily escape, pondering whether that would get me into trouble.

Gorm pushes his mouth to one side. "And you believed her?"

Feeling stupid, I say, "Judging by the look on your face, I'm guessing that wasn't wise."

The palace guard shakes his head. "I wouldn't believe a word that comes out of Loki's children's mouths any more than believing Loki."

"Oh." My cheeks burn.

We push through the palace doors and trek down the marble corridor.

Idun follows only two paces behind. "Do you think there would be any chance I could have a rest before Odin expects me to start work?"

Peering over my shoulder, I spot the dark circles under the goddess's eyes and instantly feel pity for her. With all the gods and goddesses, her job would be in high demand. She's probably been working nonstop for a long time.

I cringe with regret. "It's Odin. He's not exactly the giving or patient kind."

A black raven flies down the hall, heading directly for us. It circles over our heads a couple of times, shifting closer before returning from whence it came. I know of only two ravens that would be in the palace.

"Are they Odin's ravens?" Idun asks.

I nod. "That's either Huginn or Muninn. It's almost as though they were waiting for us and have gone to whisper into Odin's ear to let him know we're here."

The goddess sweeps her long golden-blond strands over her shoulder. "Let's hope they tell him to give us a good reception, seeing as you brought me along."

We reach a pair of wooden doors carved with intricate patterns, and Den steps aside.

"Odin is expecting you." He flings back the doors, exposing the fluttering ravens interacting with Odin before landing on the god's shoulders.

Riddled with apprehension, I step into the hall, and Idun follows, her basket of fruit swinging from her arm near her hip.

The god's eye narrows into a slit as he assesses us. "I see you've finally brought Idun."

I incline my head with respect despite his mannerisms. "Yes, I have."

Odin sits back on his throne. "I expected her a long time ago."

I straighten, clasping my hands behind my back. "There were several hiccups on the way, including a fossegrim. In case you didn't know, they can be quite hazardous to young females."

"I don't care about any fossegrim." He waves a hand dismissively. "Of course I know what they do to females. I have the gift of wisdom, and I see all." He plays with the strap of his eye patch as though to remind me he lost his eye to gain wisdom.

I play along with his arrogance, even though it's not possible for even an "all-seeing" being to see everything.

"You still should have obeyed me and brought her to me straight away. Did you not hear from the messenger, Ratatoskr?"

"Yes, I did. He passed on his usual insulting message. But like I tried to explain, we had other pressing matters we had to deal with first, and Idun wanted to help."

Idun moves as though to stand up to the god, and I discreetly shake my head at her, indicating for her to remain silent.

Odin grabs a piece of fruit off a platter on the

coffee table in front of him and drops it into his mouth. His mouth full, he tells Idun, "Frigg is waiting for you." He swallows and puts a grape into his mouth. "She is beside herself. It wasn't long ago she was distressed over something being able to kill Balder. This was relieved for a while after everything swore not to hurt him. But then something did, and she is failing to hold it together. Now she is worried about how all the stress affects her looks."

He points toward the door to one side. "Go."

Without a word, Idun curtsies then shuffles across the large marble floor, her basket rubbing against her clothes. Casting a quick glance back, she leaves me standing in the hall with Britta and Hildr by my side.

Nervously, we wait, not knowing what Odin will do next. Rarely does Odin shower us with pleasantries or satisfaction. Hildr and Britta line up against my sides, and we wait in line.

- Chapter Twenty -

We face Odin, only to be met by a giant scowl. I miss the short interval when he treated me like a worthy person, not like some incompetent Valkyrie who could never do anything right. After all, I have done great things for Asgard, and I kept my mouth shut after his mental breakdown. I bite my tongue in an attempt to refrain from retorting and making him more disappointed. I've come a long way since my time in the academy and have learned that provoking the king of the gods isn't helpful. Even so, his belittling me is getting on my nerves, and being respectful is hard. I focus on how Thor would like me to treat his father, and I attempt to uphold my leader's requests.

Rocking from one foot to the other, I watch as the ravens whisper into the god's ears.

Odin's eyebrow rises. "Is that right, Muninn?" His one eye fixes on me, cold and piercing as the raven pulls back and stands straight. "Muninn tells me that you haven't gotten all the tears that are promised to Hel in exchange for Balder's release. He tells me that there is one in particular on Jotunheim who isn't cooperating." He rubs his gray beard. "Is that true?"

Dumbfounded, I stare at the raven as he preens his feathers. How the raven would know these facts eludes me.

Hildr moves closer, back straight and head inclined. "It's my fault, great Odin. I'm the one who was responsible for that realm. I didn't get the tear from the giantess."

I shake my head at my friend. The realm wasn't hers. It was the einherjar's responsibility first. Hildr came later to help.

Odin tugs at the ear that Muninn was whispering in only moments before. "Yes, they tell me that, and that may be so. Except Kara came to help, making Jotunheim also her responsibility. She should have been able to convince the giantess to comply."

Hildr stutters. "Well, y-yes. B-but still, the giantess had already made up her mind before Kara came. Even Britta and Idun tried." This was her feeble attempt to sway the god's thoughts toward a more pleasant mindset.

"I don't care. When Kara is within your vicinity,

she is the one who is supposed to be the leader of the wingless Valkyries. She is supposed to be the prodigy under my son and to get things done. That is the reason why she is with Thor. She proved she is willing to bend over backward to get things done." He thumps his fist on his throne's armrest. "She's supposed to have the gods' interest in mind."

"And she does." Britta shifts closer to the throne, only to be shut down by a glare from Odin. Britta swallows hard, and her muscles brace in her neck and back as she readies herself to stand up to the leader of the gods. "I understand you have high expectations from Kara, great Odin. But I guarantee that Kara puts all of the gods and Asgard first. She works hard to please you and Thor."

An insect buzzes around Britta's face, and she swats it with a hand. The motion catches Zildryss's attention, and he focuses on the insect, almost going cross-eyed as he follows its progress. The insect circles my head then Hildr's. The tiny dragon's tongue licks from one eye to the other before the insect suddenly flies across the room and out of sight.

Odin clears his throat, dragging my attention away from the insect and back to the god. I'm not shocked by his glare. Yet the lump in my throat is hard to swallow.

Talking past the lump, I say, "I'm sure there are others who need to shed a tear."

Odin's glower deepens.

"I know you want everyone to shed a tear to get Balder back as soon as possible. Somehow, I find it hard to believe that everyone has done their part yet, which should mean there is still time. And we can go back to try the giantess again after we have the other tears. We aren't giving up."

Odin crosses his arms. "Let's hope so, for your sake. Otherwise, you should be tied up with Fenrir. That hound is still snapping like a rabid dog."

A rush of sadness overtakes me when I remember the hound. I still remember him as a cute puppy, and I have trouble thinking of that dog as the angry, vindictive being that blames us for punishing his father's wrongdoing. Even if Loki is free, the hound is bound to his magic tether and cannot escape. Being chained while his father is free would make him even more bitter. The anger he felt from his father's capture would change to rage over his own imprisonment.

Despite everything the hound has put us through and the threats he's made against Odin, I can't help saying, "Let's hope he settles down and becomes the friendly hound we once knew."

Odin huffs. "Your optimism never ceases to irritate me." He rises to his feet and paces. "I still expect you to get this done as soon as possible and get that tear from the giantess. Having Balder trapped in Helheim is destroying my wife."

Britta brushes my hand with hers. When our eyes meet, she indicates with her head toward the back of the hall. I follow her line of sight, the distraction a welcome relief from Odin's rambling about my incompetence. Something at the back of the hall moves, and I try to keep my face blank as I observe.

A figure is concealed behind a pillar, and I wait for it to move, following its progress in my peripheral vision, careful to appear as though I'm listening to Odin's ramblings. The figure moves slightly, exposing dark strands of hair framing a face peering around the marble. Loki's mischievous eyes lock with mine, and it takes all of my effort not to suck in a breath and keep my face plain and unemotional.

Loki twirls his fingers, and after a moment, I realize that Odin has stopped talking. The leader of the gods is holding his throat, his face red. His mouth moves, yet nothing comes out. My eyes widen. Loki must have placed a silencing spell on him. As much as I'm grateful for the silence from Odin's ramblings, I can see this going south for me. Discreetly, I connect eyes with Loki and shake my head, careful not to capture Odin's attention. Surprisingly, Loki releases

Odin's voice, and the leader's rambling continues. The pause is only acknowledged by the god's puzzled expression.

I'm not sure if Odin knows the mischievous god has been roaming the worlds, but I'm not about to be the one to let him know. He would most likely blame me, even though I've been in different realms.

Loki grins at me, and I scowl before I remember that I'm trying to remain unemotional. I attempt to wipe away the expression before Odin catches me, but I'm too late.

"How dare you scowl when I'm berating you, Valkyrie," he says.

Muninn flaps his wings, fanning Odin's shoulder-length gray hair.

"You should be listening to every word I say and apologizing for your mistakes." The king of gods starts to ramble again, scolding me for every little thing. My hands ball into fists. If I roll my eyes, that will only catch his attention. Insult after insult comes my way until I twirl my own fingers, doing precisely as I told Loki not to, and silence fills the room.

Odin clasps his throat, confusion all over his face. He's obviously trying to clear his throat, but no sound comes out. My mouth quirks, and my eyebrow twitches with amusement. Stopping him from ranting is amazingly therapeutic.

Britta discreetly runs her fingers over the top of my hand and catches my eye. She shakes her head in tiny movements. My cheeks warm as I realize I've given in to Loki's bad influence, and I release Odin's voice with a twirl of my fingers.

Odin's red face inches toward mine. "Did you hear me? I'm still waiting for your response."

I blink, trying to remember what he was saying before I made him satisfyingly silent. I don't know how he's ignoring his missing voice so quickly.

Spittle projects from his mouth as he asks, "Why aren't you apologizing for your mistakes?"

Tempted to wipe my face as the words set in, I focus on Odin with a straight face. "I apologize, great Odin. I understand that you're upset with me and wish for me to be more competent." My eyes flick back to Loki, only to see him around the side of the pillar with his thumbs up. Annoyance bubbles deep within my stomach. *How dare he approach us like this after all the trouble he has caused?* I steel my emotions and focus on Odin so that my face won't upset Odin further.

Odin tosses one hand toward the door. "Now, go and finish your chores. You shouldn't be back in Asgard. You should be gone already."

I head out the door with Britta and Hildr following me. Zildryss remains wrapped around

Britta's shoulders and peers at Loki through the Valkyrie's veil of brown hair. Loki must've been the insect flying around us earlier and knew Zildryss would expose him like he did back in Alfheim if he didn't let us know he was here.

As much as I want to race to the back of the hall and grasp the weaselly god around the neck, I don't want Odin to know he's loose. The fact that Odin didn't rave on about it makes me think he doesn't yet know. His advisers and wise ravens haven't informed him, for whatever reason.

One of Odin's ravens flaps its wings, and we quicken our pace out the door.

Chapter Twenty-One

As we follow the extensive marble corridors of Odin's palace, the noise of our scuffling boots bounces off the walls as though chasing us out.

"What was Loki doing in there?" My words are a hissed whisper. "It was like he was badgering me or us."

Hildr clenches her fists by her sides. "I don't know. It was probably to torment us. Why else would he be there?"

A black insect flies around us before circling my head and weaving its way between Britta and Hildr, capturing Zildryss's attention. The little dragon leaps to all fours and follows the insect's progress, his tongue lashing from one eye to the other. *If only the little dragon could talk.* By Zildryss's actions, I'm sure that he suspects the insect is Loki.

Hildr swipes a hand, attempting to capture the insect as it buzzes past and circles her red hair. She misses. "Oh, Vanir! The insect is really annoying me."

A sardonic smile creeps onto my face. "Try again. It could be Loki."

She swipes at it again. "What do you mean?"

Britta lunges for the insect. "This is the insect that was flying around the hall. Loki appeared in the same area, hiding behind a pillar not long after it disappeared."

Hildr's lips tighten. "That little rascal." She lunges at the insect again, trying harder to capture it, yet the insect manages to avoid her hand.

It circles out of her reach as if taunting her before heading out the door.

I take in Zildryss's wide eyes, which are still keenly focused on the place the insect went. "I wager that was Loki. Zildryss is showing the insect too much attention, and I wouldn't be the slightest bit surprised if it was him."

Sunshine streaming through the front door welcomes us outside. I acknowledge Gorm and Birger briefly before running to the dragons, who are waiting for us in the courtyard. Elan's golden face lifts my spirits in seconds, and I run a hand over her scales.

She surveys me with her golden eyes. *Any luck?*

I rest my forehead against her leg. "Only the usual berating I get from Odin."

Hildr rubs the soft part of Drogon's nose. "He still blames Kara, even though it's my fault that the giantess refused to shed a tear for Balder. He's just so pigheaded! He blames Kara for everything."

"Aren't I lucky?" I ask sarcastically.

Drogon thrashes his head from one side to the other. *Sounds like Odin needs a good horn up the backside.*

Tanda blows a raspberry. *You got that right. He's never been my favorite god, especially after what he did to all us dragons.* She rubs a cheek against Britta. *If I hadn't met this remarkable individual, I wouldn't have stayed around.*

I press against Elan's scales, soaking up the comfort of friendship. "I know. It's frustrating." I feel someone watching us and find that we are still within sight of Birger and Gorm. They catch my eye and wave, and I nod in return, glad they can't hear us. Even though they no longer mistreat us, we're currently operating under friendly observation.

Pulling away from Elan's scales, I straighten. "We should get going. As much as I'd like a good night's sleep, we have to collect these tears for Balder. If we don't finish this, I'll never hear the end of it from Odin. As much as we need to capture Loki, if he keeps fooling Odin that he's still his prisoner, he's not our first priority. Somehow, I think Loki has every intention of hiding his escape from Odin. Besides, he would probably just escape straight after his recapture."

Weaving around the castle's corner, we head toward the trees that lead us toward Yggdrasil as we leave the castle's pavement. Silence shrouds us as we ponder the task ahead.

Loki emerges from the shadows behind the castle, his shoulder-length black hair billowing in the wind. The superior, mischievous attitude on his pointy face twists a knife into my stomach, tormenting me.

I want to disable him with magic and take him back to the castle to be secured, demanding that they prohibit the shape-shifting abilities that enable him to escape. Except, I know that whatever I plan to do to him will most likely be useless. He was the teacher who taught me most of my magic, even the peaceful magic I learned on Alfheim. He's always one step ahead of me, often betraying me in different shapes and giving false friendship in other forms.

I shove the thought away and glare at him. "What is it now, Loki? Are you here to betray me some more and bring me more trouble with your mischief? You know you're the reason Odin has it in for me, don't you?"

Loki feigns hurt. "Oh, Kara. I have never, ever set out to betray you or hurt you. Besides, you've just proved that you are capable of your own mischief."

Shifting onto one leg, I cross my arms. "It was a moment of weakness."

He grins. "And I'm sure it felt good."

My eyes narrow.

He shrugs. "Besides, you're my favorite Valkyrie." He clasps his hands behind his back and approaches slowly.

I retort, "If that's how you treat your favorites, I would hate to see how you treat your least favorite Valkyrie or your enemy. I'm not surprised you have so many children through different mistresses. I can only imagine the kind of love you would give them."

"Well." His eyebrows rise with mischief. "I can see you've been taking lessons from Ratatoskr. You could improve, although your insults are getting good." He faces us with his legs apart and his hands clasped behind his back.

Elan snorts a large plume of steam over him, and he wipes perspiration from his forehead with a sleeve. *What do you want, little god? I'm sick to death of seeing you in any form. Just hurry up and let out what you want from us.*

Loki feigns hurt. "Oh, Elan. I hear that you're a

good friend to Thor, and I thought that would make me your friend too."

Elan claws at the ground. *You are wrong.*

I fish a vial out of a bag and hold it out. "You could at least shed a tear for Balder. You haven't done that yet." I shake the vial in front of him, inviting him to take it. "As much as I need to lock you up, Odin will be happy if I get a tear from you first."

Loki shies away from the vial. "Is that so?" He screws up his nose. "I don't know. The word is that Balder isn't getting released until you get a tear from everyone." He eyes the vial from a distance as though it contains an infectious disease, then he raises an eyebrow. "And you haven't gotten a tear from everyone, have you?" He rubs one black leather sleeve. "I heard in the hall that you didn't get a tear from the giantess."

Hildr moves closer to Loki. "Not yet, no. But we will." She snatches the vial out of my hand and holds it closer to the mischievous god. "So why don't you shed a tear for Balder?" She shoves it even closer, and Loki backs away, twisting his mouth to one side. "It will help with your punishment for when Odin finds out that you were the old woman who convinced Hodr to fire the mistletoe at Balder."

Loki leans on one leg and taps his other foot before crossing his arms. "No."

Stopping short of grabbing him, I let my mouth drop open. "What?"

"I said no," Loki repeats.

Chapter Twenty-Two

Hildr barely refrains from shoving the vial under his eye. "Here we go again. Acting all selfish and only thinking about yourself."

Loki waves a finger. "Don't be like that. As I have already pointed out, you haven't gathered the giantess's tears yet."

"What's that got to do with you?" Britta asks. "You could at least give something from the bottom of your heart for a change."

Loki chuckles. "I tell you what. If you get the giantess to shed a tear for Balder, I will be the first to shed a tear after her."

"I suppose you expect me to take your word for it?" I cross my arms and tap my foot. "It's not like you've kept any promise you've ever given me."

The god feigns hurt. "That's a bit harsh. I promised to teach you magic, and I did that."

"That's not what I meant, and you know it," I say.

"You've already caused me enough trouble. What's not to say that you won't break this promise too?"

Loki clasps his hands behind his back, and after pacing for a while, he pauses. "I tell you what—as part of the friendship deal…" He pauses when I roll my eyes. "I will let you capture me, and I will voluntarily walk with you to be secured inside the prison."

Britta tsks. "What's the good of that? You're only going to escape again by shape-shifting into something like an insect."

"I promise I will not shape-shift to escape. Asgard already has Fenrir tied up, and Hel knows I can escape at any time." He strokes his chin with his forefinger and thumb. "Her motives are confusing and twisted. Jormungandr is currently giving Thor a hard time." His eyes gleam. "So I think you already have enough trouble with that one."

"What's your point?" Hildr snaps.

Loki crosses his chest with a stroke of a finger. "I promise you that I will not shape-shift and escape. You have enough trouble with my children and collecting tears for Balder."

"It would have been a lot easier if you hadn't shot Balder with the mistletoe spear in the first place," Hildr says.

Loki holds a hand over his heart, appearing hurt.

"I did no such thing. I merely guided Hodr's hand as he threw the spear at his brother. He just wanted to join in the fun."

"Yes. Hodr wanted to join in the fun, not shoot his brother with the one thing that could kill him," Britta says. "Because of you, Asgard has been robbed of the best god there ever was."

"Don't I count?" Loki asks, his face serious before breaking into a cheeky grin. "Yes, yes. I know. Balder was the love of everyone's life. He was the most handsome god," he says, imitating femininity. He drops the act and continues, "I promise you I will remain behind bars until you finish collecting tears. And then I will give you the final tear from me. But I stand by my proposition. You have to get the tear from the giantess first."

I don't like this, Elan says only to me.

Me either, I respond through our bond. *I can never trust him anymore, but I'll take what I can get at this stage.* I eye Loki dubiously from head to toe. "Let's go, then." I hook my arm through his elbow. "I shall escort you to your cell."

Loki walks next to me through the courtyard and to the palace gates without hesitation. Gorm and Birger watch in disbelief and with distrust for the mischievous god as we climb the extensive stairs.

Grasping Loki's wrist firmly, I say, "It's okay, guys. I've got this. He promises not to escape."

Birger chuckles. "Yeah, right."

I worry my bottom lip. "Trust me. I know."

I march him through the marble corridors of the castle to the holding cell near where Elan was held the time Odin kidnapped her. Every guard I pass jeers as we walk toward the prison. Despite their lack of confidence, the prison guard opens the cell door, shoves Loki in, and quickly slams it shut behind him. He rattles the barred door a couple of times to ensure it's locked then ties the keys to his belt before marching to his post again.

"Stay," I tell the god as though he's a pet.

A glint sparkles in Loki's eyes. "Yes, ma'am."

I can't help what he's planning. I won't be surprised if he escapes not long after I turn my back. He has many ways to escape and get up to mischief. Despite my doubts, I turn on my heel and march out of the castle, hoping the god will do as he promises for once.

Chapter Twenty-Three

Keen to leave my distrust of Loki behind, I run down the palace steps to my friends waiting around the corner. "Let's get out of here. I want to see how Thor is doing and see if Eir needs any help gathering tears from the elves. The dark elves would make things tricky."

Elan lowers herself to the ground. *Jump on.* I hook my boot in a stirrup and lever my body up, throwing a leg over her back with ease. She rises to her feet, and I grab the reins as she launches into the air.

Following Elan's lead, the dragons, with their riders, travel through the large trunk of Yggdrasil and exit not long after into Alfheim. We stop just outside the World Tree, observing the land of the elves. It's still as beautiful as I remember, similar to Vanaheim, just not as bright. The immediate area emanates peace, reminding me how much I've missed Eir on this mission.

Zildryss lands on my shoulders unannounced, startling me. His eyes are wide as he surveys the realm before us.

I rub the bridge of his nose. "This is where you found us, isn't it?"

Briefly, he turns his big eyes to me and nods.

"Do you miss it?"

He screws up his nose then tilts his head one way then another as though thinking before shaking his head then nodding.

"Yes and no?" I ask.

He nods.

Britta interrupts. "Any ideas where to start looking for Eir?" Her eyes search the trees and the surrounding scenery.

Bubbling rivers giggle underneath us, and a large lake rests ahead. Remembering the way we went last time we were here is difficult. I was too distracted by Freyr and the way he was acting, which took my attention away from where he was leading us.

"You could start just here." The sweet voice projects from the bushes, and I glance over to see Naga's blue form approaching with Eir by his side.

"Come here, girl!" I charge forward, and despite not being a hugger, I scoop her into my arms.

Eir chuckles and hugs me in return. "I've missed you!"

Instantly, peace washes through my body like it's contagious, settling my nerves after having dealt with Odin and Loki.

Naga nudges me on his way past as he saunters toward the other dragons. The dragons have become just as connected as the four Valkyries have, and they include Zildryss in their mix. I smile when I spot Zildryss sitting on Elan's head, grabbing her horns, and looking like he's the king of the dragons.

Hildr nudges Eir on her upper arm with a fist. "It's great to see your friendly face, Eir."

Britta hugs Eir briefly, asking at the same time, "How did you do with the tears?"

Eir squeezes Britta's upper arm. "Don't worry. The residents of Alfheim have done their part. I have every tear shed. Even the dark elves were happy to cry a tear for Balder." She observes us. "How did the rest of you do?"

I adjust my belt. "Vanaheim was reasonably straightforward. But the einherjar had trouble on Jotunheim, and Hildr tried to help after completing Midgard. We tried as well, but there was one giantess that refused to cry."

With sadness on her face, Eir focuses on Hildr. "What happened?"

Running a hand through her spiky red hair, Hildr shrugs. "I completed Midgard in no time. Jotunheim was mostly easy. When I arrived to help, the giants were willing to shed a tear for the god after hearing his story. It was surprising, but all was going well until we came to one giantess. We tried several times. Britta even gave her the big sob story, trying to play to her emotions. Nothing worked. She just refused to cry." Hildr shrugs. "Even Idun, the goddess of longevity, tried bargaining with her and offering her the fruit of long life and youth in exchange. The giantess wasn't even interested. She wouldn't even half shed a tear for Balder and his untimely demise. So I failed." Hildr flicks her fingers one by one with frustration.

Eir places a hand on Hildr's shoulder. "I wouldn't say *failed*. It sounds like she's a difficult giantess. Is there anyone else who hasn't shed a tear?"

I grunt. "Yeah. Loki."

Eir's eyes instantly light up with understanding. "Do you think he'll come through?"

"I don't know. He says he will after the giantess sheds a tear. He's using her lack of cooperation as an excuse not to do it. It's so incredibly frustrating." I stamp my foot. "Although he did do one thing. He volunteered to be recaptured and to remain until we've finished collecting tears."

Eir looks surprised. "What do you think he's playing at?"

I shake my head. "I don't know. I hope he'll stick to his word this time."

"What about Thor?" Eir asks. "How did he do?"

"I don't know. If what Loki says is true, he's fighting the Midgard serpent again. We were going there to see if we could help after finding you. What about you? Did you get to catch up with your friend?"

Eir's cheeks turn a tinge of red, and she looks down at her feet. "Yes. It was lovely catching up with him. He came with me to do the rounds of Alfheim. I just said goodbye. I already miss him."

"Let's hope we'll get you back to see him soon," I say.

Naga thinks Eir needs to spend more time on Alfheim. Eir needs a mate. She is getting older all the time.

I chuckle and look into Naga's big blue eyes. "So you keep saying. I'm glad you're thinking of Eir. I know we don't live as long as dragons, but having the extended life of a Valkyrie, Eir has plenty of time to find a mate. Even so, I'm happy if she finds someone she wants to settle down with."

Naga screws up his nose. *Naga finds that hard to believe. All of you Valkyries are getting older and need a mate. Although Naga knows Kara doesn't lie to dragons, so Naga will believe Kara.*

I raise an eyebrow in disbelief that he called all of us old.

Eir cackles and rubs Naga's cheek, and he presses into her palm. "You're so funny, Naga. Calling us all old. Pfft!"

He lowers to the ground, and Eir pulls herself onto his back. We follow Eir's lead, preparing to leave the realm.

The dragons enter Yggdrasil's trunk and dive into the darkness until eventually, Elan barges out a large hole, and we enter a realm that I instantly know is Midgard. Open plains of green grass and rolling mountain peaks greet us under the beautiful blue sky. The realm's beauty hasn't diminished, even after we've seen all the realms adjoined to the Yggdrasil. Each has its own beauty, some more than others, but Midgard is much like the beauty of Vanaheim and Alfheim but with less shine. Perhaps that's because Midgard was the first realm I visited, and I will never forget how this realm shocked me with its difference from Asgard and how its beauty grabbed my heart-strings.

Drogon and Hildr exit the World Tree after us, then Eir and Naga, followed by Tanda and Britta. They line up alongside Elan, and we gaze at the sun glimmering off the ocean in the far distance.

I slip a hand under Elan's scales and use her

dragon vision to search the large body of water in front of us for the Midgard serpent and Thor, but I come up empty. "I assume we go to the water. If we don't find Thor, we may find the Midgard serpent first." I retract my hand from under Elan's scales. "I believe that the serpent has grown since we last saw him." Adjusting my uniform and pulling on my cloak, I focus on the other Valkyries. "So be alert. Thor may need our help as soon as possible."

Without waiting, Hildr yells, "Go!"

Drogon pushes into the sky with Tanda and Naga following him. My body rocks as Elan leaps into the sky after them then changes elevation to be closer to the water. With one hand grabbing her reins, I secure the cloak around me, making sure it drapes over the exposed parts of my body. Her form disappears underneath me as she turns us invisible.

Swooping low, Elan is almost dragging her talons along the water's surface. *Do you see anything?* she asks the others.

No, the dragons say in unison.

Except for the wind occasionally rippling the water, it appears to be unmoving. Elan lowers farther, the tips of her wings skimming the surface, causing urgent ripples to run from her touch.

I peer over her side and observe the disturbance, wondering if Elan made the ripples on purpose, like a signal sent to a spider through its web. Even though Elan is invisible, the thought makes me nervous, imagining the enormous Midgard serpent swimming directly toward us.

Her wings skim the water again, and my stomach drops. *Perhaps you should fly a little higher, Elan. Just in case the serpent can detect where you are from your wings disturbing the water. I'd just like to be on the safe side, in any case.*

Good thinking. Elan rises, giving us a broader view of the water beneath us, which instantly makes my shoulders relax.

The dragons and their riders fly for quite some time. Nothing indicates that Jormungandr is causing trouble, nor is there any sign of Thor. Perhaps our information is incorrect. Maybe Thor isn't on Midgard, fighting the serpent. Each flap of Elan's wings brings a strange kind of comfort that we can't find the serpent, yet at the same time, my stomach churns with worry. *What if we're too late, and the serpent has eaten the god of thunder?* I wonder.

As if in answer, a sudden bolt of lightning shoots into the sky. Unable to see Thor, I slide a hand under Elan's scales and look toward the source of the lightning. Suddenly, a large brown form ejects from the ocean, splashing water out like an explosion, then the form lands on the bank. With dragon vision, I can see it's the enormous scaly head of the Midgard serpent, bigger than a dragon. I scan it and focus on something on the bank directly in front of his nose. Thor is sprawled on his back on the ground, his hammer held high.

Chapter Twenty-Four

The enormous body of the serpent slithers farther onto the bank, his eyes fixed on the god. Thor rises to his feet and dodges to one side before falling over a rock. He scrambles backward on all fours in a crab crawl. Jormungandr's mouth opens wide, exposing his fangs and dripping black venom onto the ground.

"Get Thor!" I scream.

Elan's voice echoes mine but reaches all ears with her mind speak. *Get Thor!* Her internal voice is thunderous, and I flinch.

Instantly, Thor sees past the serpent, catching sight of the other dragons as they dive toward him. The serpent's attention is also piqued, and he removes his focus from Thor to gaze behind him. Intelligence shines in those eerie black eyes. Thor uses the opportunity to rise to his feet and gather ground. He holds up his hammer, summoning lightning and aiming it at the serpent.

The serpent turns at the last second and manages to dodge to one side, the lightning narrowly missing him. He hisses. My knees dig into the saddle as Elan plummets toward the slithering creature. Elan swoops and drags her talons across the serpent's back. His back arches, and he hisses a bloodcurdling sound, sending shivers down my spine that run to my coccyx. Shaking it off, I grab the reins more tightly as Elan swoops another time before veering up, out of reach of the Midgard serpent.

The serpent writhes with pain and twists to look for the cause. The dark eyes spot the visible dragons, and he hisses, only to be cut short as Elan swoops on his other side, dragging her talons over the scales underneath his head. The serpent spins, hissing as he dives back into the water, narrowly missed by a bolt of lightning. He lurches to one side, accidentally slamming into Elan and sending us into a spin.

As Elan regains her balance, I catch sight of Thor conjuring more lightning and aiming it at the serpent. It misses by a fraction and leaves a significant sizzled mark on the bank. The smell of burned dirt and foliage assaults my nose as Thor continues his lightning attacks, narrowly missing the water.

Lightning cracks the sky, which should be enough

to scare the serpent away for good, but he turns at the last moment, diving at the god of thunder with an open mouth. Thor sways, his energy wavering. We don't know how long he's been at this—probably quite some time. He falls over his own feet as he staggers backward, losing his hammer in the process.

Drogon dives headfirst and horns down and wedges them into Jormungandr's scales before the monster manages to obliterate the god. The serpent twists and flicks until eventually, Drogon flings to the side awkwardly. The brown dragon careens uncontrollably until Naga dives into his path, grabs Drogon's tail in his mouth, and counters his rotation with his flight to stabilize the brown dragon's flight. When Drogon's spinning slows, he angles his wings to brace himself and regain control of his flight.

Pale-faced, Hildr grips Drogon's reins, her knuckles white.

Tanda dives like a red streak, shooting a long plume of fire and scorching the exposed side of the serpent's scales. Still invisible, Elan attacks from behind, scraping her talons along the serpent's back and cutting deep gashes along his body.

Jormungandr screeches, hurting my ears, before he retreats into the water.

Thor calls for his hammer and sends it after the serpent, clipping him on the chin and making him lodge his fangs into his own flesh. The god of thunder calls to the hammer with his hand extended, and it returns like a boomerang and lands neatly in his palm. He spins and tosses the hammer again. The serpent narrowly dodges the blow as he wriggles backward, squirming until all his brown scales disappear under the ocean's surface.

Thor catches his hammer then calls to Hildr, "Keep an eye on him."

Sill pale, Hildr fails to respond, but Drogon nods and flicks his tail, flying just above the water's surface and pursuing the serpent's progress.

Naga flies beside the brown dragon while Zildryss wraps around Eir's shoulders. They follow the ripples disturbing the water's surface, and Naga pays particular attention to the bubbles rising from deep within the ocean.

Thor stumbles, holding his shoulder, and waves away my offer of healing as Elan lands next to him. He turns to Elan, "We need to keep an eye on him to see where he goes next." He pauses and takes a few deep breaths. "The serpent has to be tamed once and for all."

That's precisely what Drogon and Naga are doing. Elan's tone is friendly yet slightly berating in a way that only Elan can get away with. *Now, hold still, and let us assist you.*

Studying Thor, I look for any sign of injury. Scrapes and bruises cover nearly every part of his exposed flesh—over his face and down his arms.

"Are you okay?" I ask, not finding any signs of any severe damage.

He rubs a patch on his forehead that's bulging into a large lump hiding under his auburn hair, and he nods. "Sure. I'm as good as can be. Thanks for coming to help. That thing is enormous now."

Lifting his red locks, I observe the lump. "I noticed." I place my hands on the different injuries and begin healing him.

A loud thud behind me makes me spin around. Tanda lands, and Britta slides off her saddle.

Britta marches toward Thor. "Did you manage to get the tears from the under realms?"

One side of Thor's mouth pushes into a grimace. "Nice to see you too." He straightens and draws back his shoulders, his face withering in pain. "Out of the living, all of Niflheim and Helheim are done. All the living in both those realms and Muspelheim were keen to shed a tear for Balder. I found that disconcerting, but I took them without question, as we are on a mission to save my brother. I was checking Midgard on my way up to the top when Jormungandr decided to rear his ugly head and attack. He must've heard that I was in the realm. He came out of nowhere, terrorizing the people living along the shoreline of the village I was visiting at the time." He observes Britta from under one raised eyebrow. "How about you? Did you get all the tears?"

Her brow pushes together. "So far, we have managed to get everyone to shed a tear except for one giantess on Jotunheim. Oh, and of course, Loki is being difficult." Spite laces her voice.

Thor huffs and crosses his arms. "Of course. He always has to stir the pot in the wrong direction."

"He promises to shed a tear after the giantess." As soon as the words leave my mouth, I feel stupid.

Thor asks the question taunting me in the back of my mind. "Are you sure the giantess isn't Loki in disguise?"

My head goes numb, and I gather all my courage to look my leader in the eye. "I'm beginning to wonder." I resist the urge to slap my forehead. "I admit there was something familiar about her."

Thor shakes his head. "If history is anything to go by…"

I expel a long sigh. "Let's hope you're wrong."

Zildryss unexpectedly glides into our group and lands on Thor's shoulder before wrapping around his neck.

Thor chuckles. "Hello, little guy. Nice to see you again."

The little lilac dragon presses against the god's neck before settling down.

A loud thump sounds behind me as Drogon lands with Hildr on his back, and Naga lands shortly thereafter.

Hildr's face is torn with anguish. "We have bad news."

"What is it?" Thor asks.

Hildr's shoulders stiffen. "The serpent has decided to leave Midgard and enter Yggdrasil."

Instantly, Thor's face pales. "What? I didn't think that was possible." Long lines crease his forehead.

Eir's normally peaceful face is torn with anguish. "I'm afraid it is. My guess is that he's probably heading to Asgard."

"Are you sure?" Thor asks. "Asgard has hardly any rivers."

Hilda shrugs. "Unfortunately, it looks that way. I wasn't about to be stuck in the World Tree with him. There's not enough room to maneuver. Although one thing is certain: we need to find him."

Thor lets out an exasperated sigh and shakes his head. "I don't blame you. We have to stop him." He dusts off his leggings and jerkin. "Are you ready to go?"

Elan squats, ready for me to climb on. *We certainly are.*

Wearily, I climb onto her back and invite Thor to sit behind me with a wave of a hand. I yank him up by an arm, and he throws a leg over Elan's back. Within a few moments, Elan and the other dragons push into the air and aim for Yggdrasil in an attempt to stop the Midgard serpent.

THE END

ACCOSTED: book 8 in Thor's Dragon Rider series can be found on Amazon.

IF YOU ENJOYED ASSIGNED, please take a few minutes and leave a review on Amazon. Thank you. Reviews help authors.

Get updates & notifications of giveaways

Would you like a FREE ebook?

Click here to get started: FREE copy of Wolf Heart: Fenrir's Journey to Asgard or go to https://BookHip.com/KQGGZF

Through this link you can sign up for my newsletter and

receive a FREE copy of Wolf Heart plus updates about my fantasy books, sales and notification of giveaways.

ACKNOWLEDGMENTS

Thank you to all of the creators of literature and websites who have spent time writing about Norse Mythology. Even though at times there has been contradicting information, it has been an interesting study. After all, of course a goat produces mead, and a dragon gnaws at the roots of the Yggdrasil, unhindered, threatening the existence of the nine realms attached to the world tree. Plus, there are many other "believable" tales told.

Norse mythology is such an impressive set of tales that I have incorporated some and invented others to create Kara and Elan's story.

I am touched by the enormous amount of support I have received from my immediate family. My husband has been a helpful first reader and, at times, been an excellent motivator, with hints of ideas to help me through the blanks. The support from my three sons has also been overwhelming. They have spent years putting up with my head in the clouds, thinking about the next plot twist or story, along with many hours spent working on my books and keeping in touch with my readers.

A big thank you to my extended family, who support me being a book enthusiast.

A huge thank you to my editor, Kelly Reed, for her editing and writing tips, and my proofreader, Sussie B., for picking up the things we missed.

Thank you to all of my readers who have loved my work, and continue to read my stories.

BOOKS BY KATRINA COPE

Pre-Teen Books

The Sanctum Series

JAYDEN'S CYBERMOUNTAIN

SCARLET'S ESCAPE

TAYLOR'S PLIGHT

ERIC & THE BLACK AXES

ADRIANNA'S SURGE

~~~~~

Young Adult Urban Fantasy

Afterlife Series

FLEDGLING

THE TAKING

ANGELIC RETRIBUTION

DIVIDED PATHS

TRUTH HUNTER

Afterlife Novelette

THE GATEKEEPER

~~~~~

Young Adult Urban Paranormal Fantasy

Supernatural Evolvement Series

(Associated with the Afterlife Series)

WITCH'S LEGACY (Prequel)

AALIYAH

~~~~~

Young Adult Norse Mythology Fantasy

Valkyrie Academy Dragon Alliance

MARKED (Prequel)

CHOSEN

VANISHED

SCORNED

INFLICTED

EMPOWERED

AMBUSHED

WARNED

ABDUCTED

BESIEGED

DECEIVED

Thor's Dragon Rider

SAFEGUARD

PURSUIT

ENTRAPMENT

HOODWINKED

RELINQUISHED

SHROUDED

ASSIGNED

ACCOSTED

DESTRUCTION

ABOUT THE AUTHOR

Katrina is a best-selling author of young adult fantasy and middle grade / tween novels. Her novels incorporate action, heart and an intriguing plot.

She resides in Queensland, Australia. Her three teenage boys and husband for over twenty years treat her like a princess. Unfortunately though, this princess still has to do domestic chores.

From a very young age, she has been a very creative person and has spent many years travelling the world and observing many different personalities and cultures. Her favourite personalities have been the strange ones, yet the ones under the radar also hold a place in her heart.

Katrina's online home is at www. katrinacopebooks.com

You can connect with Katrina on:

Facebook Group

facebook.com/Author.Katrina.Cope

twitter.com/Katrina_R_Cope

instagram.com/katrina_cope_author

pinterest.com/katrinacope56

bookbub.com/profile/katrina-cope